The Secret of Blue Lake
By: Marcy Blesy

This book is a work of fiction. Names, characters, places, and events are a result of the imagination of the author or are used fictitiously. Any resemblance to actual persons, living or dead, businesses, events, or locations is a coincidence.

No part of the text may be reproduced without the written permission of the author, except for brief passages in reviews.

Copyright © 2023 by Marcy Blesy, LLC. All rights reserved. Cover design by Cormar Covers

Chapter 1

"There's a pile up on the Dan Ryan," says my boss Jerry Stanley, his excitement for the craziest of news stories on full display. "A milk tanker collided with a truck carrying cocoa powder." He laughs, a deep hearty laugh that fills the newsroom. "I can't make this stuff up."

"Headlines writing themselves, huh?" I shake my head. It's never a dull moment at WDOU.

"Chocolate Milk Causes Road Closure on Busy Chicago Interstate," he says, smiling.

"Take a crew and talk to some people if you can—witnesses and drivers."

"Are there any fatalities?" It's the worst part of my job. Covering deaths is never easy, but since Mom died it's nearly impossible.

"No fatalities, Meg." He pats me on the shoulder. "Now get going. Take Brian with you. He needs to learn his way around Chicago," says Jerry.

I roll my eyes. The last thing I want to do is take our newest reporter Brian Welter *anywhere*. Before I can protest, I feel Brian's presence, his stale hidden-but-not-hidden cigarette stench permeating from his suit jacket.

"Meggin Popkin!" He slaps the wall outside Jerry's office. "I hear I'm hanging with the number one street reporter."

I groan. No one calls me *Meggin* anymore. In a world full of Jennifers, Michelles, and Kristis, my parents bucked the trend and named their second child Megan, a different but regular-enough sounding name that they spelled M-E-G-G-I-N. I can appreciate their quest for originality, but with everyone spelling my name wrong, it was simpler to call myself Meg.

"Earth to Meggin!" Brian shouts through his cupped hands. No one should be allowed to yell at another person so closely unless in the throes of passion.

I wince at the sound of his annoying voice, ignore him, and head to my cubicle. He follows, landing in step with me. The news station abounds with energy and business, always with something going on in the Chicagoland area: the sounds of fingers on keys punching out stories or answering emails, the police scanners blaring, waiting to point a reporter to a new crime to cover, and the faint sound of elevator music playing through the overhead speakers that aim to calm the anxieties of the stories covered here.

"I'll meet you by the station van," I say. "I need to grab my phone."

"It's okay. I can wait for you. We can share an elevator. Go ahead and fix your hair, too, of course."

I know he's smiling a nauseating grin without even seeing his face. I've met this kind. I almost married this kind once before when I was young and dumb. Now I know better. But I don't get asked my opinion about new on-air talent. Even though Brian Welter comes with accolades galore for his on-air presence in Tucson, his *in-person* presence is nothing short of arrogance.

I ignore Brian as I grab my jacket along with my phone while shutting down my laptop. I have a superstition about leaving my computer on when I'm not at my desk. I don't want anyone seeing a story before it's buffed up and ready for its audience.

Brian stands to the side of the hallway as I brush past him. He rushes by to push the elevator button like a little boy fighting with his sister over who gets to push all the buttons. When Lara and I were little, we'd been assigned days. I got to do the "things" on even-numbered days while Lara got to do them on the odd-numbered days. Mom said that system cut our arguments in half. Something tells me Brian was an only child who never learned the value of compromising or perhaps the oldest who always thinks he's right. I can't help but glance in the elevator mirror before the door opens, making sure my bangs are aligned and no strands of my shoulder-length brown hair have parted on their own accord. Satisfied, I slide out the door before Brian.

Brian reaches the station van first and grabs the passenger seat door handle before I can stop him.

"No, you don't," I say, slapping my hand on the door handle, too.

"There's not room for both of us, kid." He brushes my hand away as he slips into the van.

"What an ass." I slam the backseat door.

"You'd better not mess with Meg, man," says Tom. We make eye contact through the rearview mirror. You don't make friends at a news station by ruffling the feathers of the cameraman.

"Her? I think I can handle *Meggin,*" he says, laughing.

"I don't need *handling.* Drive, Tom." Tom accelerates so quickly that Brian's phone slides off the dashboard and crashes into the door.

"Dammit, Tom!" he says as he reaches for his phone.

Tom, our cameraman, has been recording my news segments since I first came to WDOU five years ago. Tom and I are more than work associates. We are friends. He and his wife, Anita, were the first people in line at Mom's visitation when she died. He still brings me leftovers once a week, either extra meat he'd grilled with a side of potatoes or an extra portion of stir fry. Tom cares for me like a little sister. I know he's got my back.

I put in my AirPods before I can hear more of Brian's drivel. I watch the busy city streets pass by as we race to the scene of the chocolate milk interstate. It's easy to imagine myself living on one of those little side streets living the life of a school librarian like I'd grown up thinking I'd be. Walking the stacks, looking for the perfect alphabetical placement, sneaking in readings of newly published books. There are days when I wished I'd never gone with Dad to his job at the newspaper, when management had called for a reporter to cover the local school board meeting, and he'd looked at me and asked his boss to let me go because no one wanted the gig. And I'd gone. And I'd fallen in love with telling stories, stories of boring school board meetings to stories of convenience store break-ins to stories of interstate pileups. But some days I still wonder what it would be like living the privacy of a librarian's job without being critiqued for every outfit choice or inadvertent nose booger.

Tom grabs his camera after finally finding a place to park in a back alley between Garfield and S. Wentworth Avenue. We take the chance of getting towed, and it wouldn't be the first time. The station budgets for such expenses. *Get to the story first. Worry about the van second.*

It's a hike up the embankment to the interstate. No one should get twenty feet within distance of a Chicago interstate under normal circumstances, the cars flying miles over the speed limit, weaving in and out of traffic. But no one is moving today. I count fifteen cars that have experienced some bit of fender or bumper damage, the highway beneath our feet a cloudy brown color mixing the cocoa powder from one over-turned semi-trailer with the milk of another. I toss a glance at the side streets below the interstate and wonder again why I'm not living the life of a single librarian. It might not seem glamorous, but to me it sounds perfect right about now. The early spring temperatures in Chicago make me shiver involuntarily. I hope the chocolate milk washes away the dirty snow that lines the road. Only the first winter snow in Chicago is welcome. Every snow after lingers as a mess of dirt and trash and pollution alongside the streets for months until the temperatures warm up long enough for fresh rains to wash it away.

"Meg, you have a perspective yet?" asks Tom. He rests a camera on his shoulder and points at the scene before us, a mess of banged up-cars and trucks with people on their phones and milling around the scene talking with police and other emergency workers.

"Yeah, sorry. I'll start with that blue car. It's the closest one to the cocoa powder truck." I point to a large white truck with pictures of chocolate bars on the side. I remember that I haven't eaten lunch today. The truck is on its side, the back half blocking the right lane of traffic and the back door swung open with punctured containers of cocoa powder spilling out. The milk truck it collided with is also on its side, in the adjoining left lane with its back door open, too. Milk continues to drip down and out the truck and into the cocoa powder below.

Tom starts to follow me as I weave between cars heading to the young woman who is leaning against her car and talking on the phone. Her compact car rests against the side of the road with a bumper that looks like a large accordion after making what looks like impact with the back tire of the cocoa powder truck.

I flash my station credentials in front of her. She drops the phone to her side.

"Excuse me, miss. I'm Meg Popkin with WDOU. I'd like to ask you a few questions."

She looks at Tom who is directing his camera at her. "Okay. I can talk," she says, brushing her hands through her long brown hair, a not-so-subtle attempt to be camera ready. "I…I've been crying," she says as she looks at the camera.

I smile reassuringly. "I imagine you have. It's been a scary day."

She smiles, too, comforted by the first in-person contact she's had since the accident. "I'm Quinn," she says.

Quinn answers my questions, becoming visibly calmer as I finish learning about the accident and its effect on her. She'd been talking to her boyfriend on the phone—hands free, of course—when the collision had occurred from behind, sending her sliding into the back of the semi-truck. She's relaxed enough to laugh about the absurdity of the mess that covers the interstate. "I guess all we need now are some cookies," she says amused with her own wit.

I thank her for her time and turn to leave when Brian grabs the microphone from my hand. I hadn't even noticed he was standing behind me. "What the...?" I ask.

"Quinn, when will you be filing your lawsuit?" he asks, thrusting the microphone so close to Quinn's face it nearly knocks out a tooth.

"A what?" She wrinkles her nose and looks at me.

"Give me back my microphone," I say, trying to yank it from Brian's firm grip.

He pulls it away and back into Quinn's face. "A lawsuit," he repeats. "You stand to make a lot of money from this accident, you know?"

"I...I don't want money. I want my car fixed and to move on. This has been the scariest day of my life." She looks at me, any sense of calmness disappearing from her face.

"Shut off the camera," I say to Tom. He glances at Brian who is giving him a stink eye while shaking his head back and forth. "Shut it off, Tom," I repeat.

Tom nods his head and pulls the camera from his shoulder. He knows who the boss is here. "Thanks, Quinn.

11

Sorry about my associate. Best wishes to you." I walk away. Tom follows.

After speaking with the driver of the milk truck and another driver who'd witnessed the collision, I'm still angry with Brian. I stomp through the chocolate milk and dirty snow back to the embankment. I sidestep my way down the hill but lose my footing on a slippery patch of snow and finish my trek down the hill on my butt. I try to stand up right away, but I slip again, this time falling forward. My pants are soaking wet. My hands are muddy, and I've lost a shoe. My day keeps getting better.

Brian arrives first at the scene of *my accident* which surprises me since he'd left my shadow after trying to mess up my interview with Quinn, his reporter's notebook hanging out of his back pocket. He doesn't hold in his laughter as he jogs down the hill behind me. "You really know how to make an exit," he says. "Here, grab my hand." He reaches his hand out to me.

I slap it away and accept Tom's help when he's rejoined us after filming more images but not shots with Brian in them. "Are you okay, Meg?" he asks, pulling me to my feet.

"I'm fine," I say too cheerily, "Nothing damaged!"

"But how's your ego?" Brian asks as he hands me my shoe.

"My *ego* is solid though not as large as yours." I stomp through the dirty snow as quickly as I can to get back to the van first and grab hold of the passenger door. Tom throws me an old towel for the front seat, and I slam the door shut behind me before Brian can reply. Still, I have to give it to Brian to find another way to get the story even when the cameraman had taken my side for the day. We don't talk all the way back to the station.

"Send the tape to editing," Jerry says when I walk into the station. "We're going to run it on the 5:30 news. What took you guys so long?" he asks before seeing my muddy clothes. "What happened to you, Meg?" His eyes are as big as teacup saucers. Jerry is a great boss. Part of being a great boss it making sure things are done right and on time. And *without incident,* his favorite phrase when out on assignment.

"She bruised her bum, apparently, but not her ego, Jerry. This one's a tough cookie," Brian says gleefully.

I glare at him.

"Jerry, I have the best stories to tell," says Brian.

I purse my lips and stare at Brian. He's smiling so widely that his perfect teeth look like they'll pop out of his mouth with one swing.

"You went on camera?" Jerry asks, raising an eyebrow in surprise and ignoring my appearance for a moment.

"Well, actually I like to talk to my sources *off camera* first. Then I record my reflections on camera when I get back to the station. The camera intimidates sources from talking when they've been through something traumatic," he says, smiling as fake as the eyelashes on a Hollywood starlet.

I want to vomit from the acridness of his words. Plus, I really want to clean up and change clothes.

"So, I think I'll use the stationary camera I saw in the back offices to record my segment for tonight's news."

"That is ridiculous!" I can't hold back. "Jerry, I have a witness on camera who gave me an awesome interview. I talked to the driver of the milk truck. That's all we need along with Tom's shots of the scene. This isn't a major story, after all. We don't need Brian to do *anything*."

Jerry looks between Brian and me. I know he's weighing his options—keeping me happy and accommodating the new guy. "Hmm…Brian, go ahead and record your piece. Meg, take Brian's segment to editing with your segment." He sighs and curses under his breath. "You know I'm not happy about this. It's going to put us right up to news time. You are both making my job harder. If you learn to play nicely, things will be a lot easier for *all* of us." He walks away a few steps before adding. "You have 45 minutes. No exception. And clean yourself up, Meg! You look a mess!"

I death stare at Brian who has the audacity to laugh out loud. "If you play nice, you get what you want. You heard Jerry, Meg. Seems like you need to learn how to be nice. Grab a drink with me tonight, and I'll teach you how to be nice." He winks at me.

"I'd rather drink alone for the rest of my life than ever go out with you."

He snorts out loud and covers his mouth with a sickening giggle. "*That,* my dear, is not a stretch to imagine. Enjoy your solitude."

"You have fifteen minutes to get your part to me or the editing department won't have time to mesh it with mine!" I spit out before Brian saunters away.

I watch him walk away to record his story—my story—and dream about taking off my low black pump and throwing it at his head.

Chapter 2

I knock lightly and wait for Dad to answer the door. It's our once-a-month Tuesday date night. Donuts with Dad, Daddy-Daughter Dances—all have been a part of my life growing up. With as busy as Mom was in all of her community commitments from quilting club to museum volunteer to herb society president, Dad was the parent of consistency. He made sure a parent would be home to help Lara and me with homework or to run us to our own commitments. But now these dad-daughter times are more for Dad than for me. Lara and I noticed quickly after Mom's death that Dad stopped doing things—not just things like going to social functions or his grandsons' events—but things like doing his laundry or cleaning the kitchen or even getting out of bed some days. It was scary. Our strong, capable father fell apart without our mother. Her very presence gave him life.

She'd been his pride and joy since seventh grade when Mom had talked her way into being the stats keeper for the boys' basketball team, something girls had never been allowed to do before. But that was Mom. She wanted something, and she did whatever she could to get it. Lara has that talent, too. She should have been the on-air personality in the family.

Later on, Mom pivoted her ability from getting things done around the home to seeing needs in our community and working her charm to accrue resources to fix the issues: raising money to help convert an old building into small apartments for low-income housing, helping to install a dog park in a congested area with little grass, arranging for rides for patients who needed to get to the hospital for chemo or dialysis, even for people who were strangers to sit with those people during their procedures. When Mom went through her own chemo, she never lacked friends who practically stepped over each other to be the one to sit with *the one* who had been there for so many.

Though the visitation line at Mom's funeral snaked around the funeral home and out the door with gads of community members who wanted to offer their condolences and to tell their stories of their time with Mom, no one grieved her more than Dad.

The door opens, and my handsome, lightly gray-haired father stands before me with arms outstretched. "Meg, it's so nice to see you." His genuine glee to see me is comforting after a long day.

I look around the room, happy to see not a stitch of disorder. He's worked so hard to treat his depression. When Lara and I had recognized the effects of his grief, we'd intervened. Dad hadn't argued. The therapy had been helpful as had his acceptance of help from us and a housekeeper, of course.

But when I turn the corner in the living room to get a glass of wine from the kitchen, I stop short in my tracks. "Dad, what are you doing?" The kitchen counters and island are full: glasses, plates, bowls, pots, pans. Open cabinet doors highlight empty shelves. "Are you rearranging your kitchen?" I ask. I open the refrigerator, pull out an opened bottle of pinot and pick a wine glass off the counter to fill.

"Let's sit down, Meg, okay?" Dad asks.

"What's going on?" I don't like small talk. Get to the point. Don't allow time for my mind to fill in the blanks. I follow Dad into the living room. I push aside a yellow pillow, an attempt by Lara to brighten Dad's mood with brightly colored accessories. "What's going on?" I ask again.

"First, tell me about your day. You look tired," he says, patting my knee.

I know better than to press. As much as *I* need to know what's going on, my genial father won't tell me until I've told him my problems first. "There's a new reporter at the station." I sigh and take a drink.

Dad raises his eyebrow. "A dating possibility?"

"Dad, I'm not in college. I'm almost thirty! You can't ask me these things anymore. It's insulting. I don't need to date everyone new that I meet. Plus, this guy's a real ass, a showboat type with no respect." I pick a piece of lint from my yoga pants and hope the conversation topic will change.

"Of course, Meg. I'm sorry. I want you to be happy." He smiles and I melt, like I have my whole life when my dad smiles, his eyes twinkling despite the wrinkles that surround them.

"I want to be happy, too. I *am* happy."

"Good, Meg. I'm glad you're happy."

I take a deep breath and another drink of wine. My dad never got over my breakup with Will. He'd been fine enough to date when it was only the two of us, but he had a lot of traits that, honestly, remind me of Brian: show-off in public, out storying the next guy's stories. I got tired of the stories. I got tired of the attention seeker. I didn't *hate* Will.

I just grew to dislike him greatly, in fact. Dad has never gotten over it. If Will knew how to do one thing well, it was how to woo my dad. Mom had loved him, too. He worked both of my parents well. But if they'd heard the way he criticized them behind their backs calling *their* goodness holier-than-thou, they'd have been crushed. So, I never told them. I just let him go. And I've never looked back.

"Can we get back to why your kitchen looks like you're doing an early spring clean?"

"Okay, Meg. I'll tell you." He pauses for a moment before crushing my world. "I'm moving."

"Moving?" I sip my wine and try to organize my thoughts. "Okay, I guess…I mean….I guess that makes sense. There are a lot of memories of Mom in the house. It must be hard. And the house is big, too big for a single man. I understand," I try to convince myself out loud. "I understand. Have you found something smaller? A condo? Maybe within walking distance to stores and restaurants? I wish you'd let Lara and me help you."

Dad stops my ramblings by putting a hand on my knee. "Meg, I'm leaving the state."

I blink in confusion. "*The state?*"

"Yes, but not too far. I'll be three hours away in Michigan." His eyes light up as if it is the most natural thing in the world that my dad who has two daughters, a son-in-law, and three grandsons within thirty minutes of each other on a good traffic day in the Chicagoland area that we've lived in for our entire lives would decide to up and pack everything he owns to move three hours away.

But it is not natural. It is not right. "Why, Dad? Why would you leave us?" I ask, squeezing my eyes shut so that I do not cry.

"I need a change."

"I get that, Dad. I really do. But why Michigan? Why so far away?"

He coughs and wipes his nose with the back of his hand. "It's a lovely community. I've done my research. I think I will be very happy there. I think it will be the best thing for all of us."

"The best thing? You'll miss so much. The boys are growing up. Don't you want to be able to see their soccer games? Or baseball? And Lara and Rick need a babysitter. You're the best babysitter, Dad. And I need you…"

"Stop, Meg. I'm not leaving the family. This is *good* for the family. Trust me. This is what needs to happen. And you can visit. I *want* you to visit."

People always thought Mom was the force for change in the family. But though she was exceptional at getting things done, it's Dad who can make a decision with consequences that have been thought out completely, with no amount of second-guessing needed—at least in his mind. I know there is nothing more that can be done. He is leaving. Now only one question remains. "When?" I whisper.

"Next weekend. The moving truck comes on Saturday."

Chapter 3

"I don't understand this at all," says Lara as she runs a roll of tape over yet another box, forty years' worth of Mom and Dad's things making the move to Michigan. She blows a strand of her long brown hair out of her eyes, a missed piece from her messy bun.

My sister Laramie, who appreciated my parents' spelling of her name, should have been the on-air talent in our family, not me. She has the flare for the dramatic, but she's sunk her skills into raising the best family in the Midwest. And she's done a good job. Her husband Rick is a successful software developer. They have three children, all boys, who excel at every extracurricular activity they try. While we couldn't be more different, we'd become united in our desire to keep Dad from slipping into further depression. And we'd done a good job.

"He is definitely being weird," I say. I wrap another wine goblet for the move. "Does he really need a whole set of these anymore?" The boxes pile around us, the memories of our parents' lives being condensed to various sized cubes.

"Who knows what he needs?" She pauses to wind up the toy sitting at her feet for my nephew Nolan. He giggles without a care in the world. If only life could be that simple for the rest of us.

"I talked to him before he left for the gym. He told me it would be for the *good* of the family. What the hell does that mean?" She shoots an eye at Nolan who is oblivious to his mother's swearing. "Doesn't he know how much he is going to miss with his grandsons? Blake and Owen have soccer and Cub Scouts. And karate lessons? I do *not* understand. Ever since Mom died, he's been different."

I sink into Dad's easy chair, an overgrown monstrosity that he and Mom argued over but that he swore was the most comfortable piece of furniture he's ever had the pleasure of sitting upon. I have to agree. It's pretty comfortable. "Lara, he's different because Mom *died*. You have to cut him some slack."

Lara wipes away a tear with the back of her hand. Nolan throws me a squishy ball. I throw it to him, but he misses, crawling after it like a puppy. "Our whole lives have changed," she says.

"Yep, but you have Rick and the boys. You'll be fine." I look out the bay window in the family room next to the kitchen. Mom's prized violets are in full bloom, dotting her flowerbed along the fence line with a burst of variations of purple.

Lara drops to the floor and picks up Nolan who dutifully sits on her lap. "You'll be fine, too, Sis. Tell me about the new guy at work. Dad mentioned something about it. Are you interested?"

I kick my foot in the air as I get up from Dad's chair. *"That* is the most ridiculous question ever. The new reporter at work is an arrogant ass. I am most definitely *not* interested. Why does everyone in this family think that every new guy that crosses my path should be a dating interest?"

"Sorry. It's a natural question. You aren't getting any younger, you know?"

I let out a little scream that startles Nolan who covers his face. "Sorry, buddy," I say. "Your mom's a little cuckoo."

"Cuckoo. Cuckoo," he says.

Lara rolls her eyes. "Thanks for that."

"It's your fault. You started it."

"Fine, then tell me how work is going." She starts piling books into a box.

"It's okay. I'm getting a bit burned out with all of the mundane stories." I remove pictures from the wall. The middle school years were not kind to me. Braces *and* glasses were a hard *no* on the self-esteem meter.

"Are there any other stories you could cover? You *do* work at a news station in a major metropolitan network, you know."

"I know that. I'd love to do special features, stories that are more than 60 seconds—something with heart."

Nolan claps his hands.

Lara and I chuckle. "Well, Nolan thinks that is a good idea for Aunty Meg."

"I wish Nolan was my boss."

Chapter 4

"But, Jerry, come on! I can do it. I was a newspaper writer before starting at the station. Let me tell stories with meaning." I plead my case as I refill my boss's coffee cup, hoping for an empathetic ear. He shuffles papers on his desk as if I'll think he's busy. I don't.

"Meg, if you like telling stories with *heart* as you say, then go back to the newspapers. Hell, write for magazines. You'll get a lot more words there. But we need you out there in the streets. No one knows Chicago like you do. This station is teeming with reporters, but you're always my go-to reporter when there is a breaking story or something extra important to cover. You're the face of this city. People trust you when they see you and hear you on the streets." He takes the coffee cup from my hand. "Plus, Gordan's been our features reporter. I can't exactly tell the guy that's been writing the *feely* stories for fifteen years that I'm replacing him, can I?" Jerry takes a sip of his coffee before setting it down on his desk.

"I'm not asking you to replace Gordan with me," *though there is something to be said about news reporters getting stale if they never change their approach to stories* I want to say. "Give me a chance to tell some feature stories, too. Plus, you have

28

Brian now. That should give me more time to do other kinds of stories."

"Brian's still learning his way around the city. And there might be other things in store for Brian." He talks quietly as he trails off the end of his sentence. He rearranges his pen container as he avoids eye contact with me.

I arch my eyebrows in disbelief. "Are you saying that Brian is going to be an *anchor*?"

"I'm saying there might be some shake up in the office over the next year or so. I'm keeping my options open. It's not some big secret that our ratings are dipping."

"So, let me help. Let me tell some really great stories. I guarantee it will improve ratings, Jerry."

This time it's Jerry's turn to be skeptical. *"Guarantee?"*

"Give me a chance to find a really great story to tell. Let me find a Chicagoland story that makes people happy, gives them hope."

"I'll consider it. Now finish editing your story about the bank. We need it for the 5:30 news." He waves me out of the office. "And thanks for the coffee."

"No thanks to you," I mumble as I leave his office.

"What was that?" he yells after me.

"Nothing!"

"Hey, girl!"

I turn around from my cubicle chair when the polished voice that likely works on the desperate women of the world invades my space. "Don't call me that," I hiss. "You know my name."

"Ah, yes, that's right. *Meggin*."

"My name is Meg," I say, turning back to my computer to add the details to my story of the old woman who mistook the accelerator for the brake and crashed into a bank on Harlem Avenue. The woman was fine, the brick wall of the bank—not so much.

"Listen, I heard your conversation with Jerry…"

I pivot around in my chair. "You were *listening* to my conversation, you mean?"

"Yeah, I guess you could say that. Anyway, if you want to write more stories with heart or whatever goofy woman-feeling angle you're going for, you have to bring the story *to* Jerry. Guys like Jerry don't assign stories like that. You have to do your research; find something he'll like.

30

Write it up. Give him the full picture. Sell it to him *after* you have the story."

I squint at Brian—tall, athletic, handsome to some—with wavy blonde hair and green eyes. But at this moment I see nothing but ugliness when I look at him.

"Come for drinks with me after work. I'll explain what I mean."

I roll my eyes. "I'm a quick learner. I understand." I rotate in my chair back to the computer.

Brian moves so that he is standing directly over my computer screen. "One drink. Then you can go. I really do know what I'm talking about. Plus, I'll make you a deal. Come for a drink, and I'll put in a good word for you with Jerry."

I stand up, grabbing my suit jacket. "And why would Jerry listen to anything you have to tell him? You're the *new* guy."

"Exactly. I'm the *new guy* who he hand-picked from Tucson to come to Chicago to breathe some life into this failing station. I know what I'm talking about. And you should listen to me."

After the 10:00 news where I again shared my interview with the poor bank teller who'd nearly been run over by the old woman, I take my backpack to the bathroom to change. The last thing I want to do is have a drink with Brian Welter, but if he can bend Jerry's ear to my desires, then one drink can't hurt, at least that's what I hope. I change into my train clothes. No one recognizes me on the 'L'—Chicago's elevated train—or the Metra train I take to the western suburbs when I'm wearing yoga pants and a baggy sweatshirt. Tonight's ensemble of navy-blue yoga pants and an oversized University of Illinois sweatshirt is the perfect drinking attire, even if I'm not in my apartment doing it alone.

I walk out of the station and next door to Henry's, a laid-back dive favored by the locals. There are enough people crowding the bar to blend in, and the locals don't bother with things like celebrity or whatever attention you'd call it that Chicago reporters sometimes attract when out in other parts of the city. When I open the door to Henry's Bar, Brian stands up and yells across the room. "Hey, Meggin—over here!"

A group of equal parts gym rat and couch potato former athletes double over as if Brian has likely said something disparaging about my appearance. Good, that's exactly what I wanted. I nod my head in their direction before walking to the bar to order a drink. Before I can get the bartender's attention, Brian's yelling over my shoulder.

"Scotch for the lady," he yells.

I hate this guy. And I don't drink Scotch. "Make that a pinot!" The bartender grabs a wine glass. Is it odd that I find this win slightly gratifying?

"Settle down, Meggin," Brian says as he sits on the bar stool next to where I am standing. "I invited you, so the least I can do is get you a drink. The *pinot* is on me." He pulls out his wallet, revealing a wad of cash, likely a twenty surrounding nothing but ones.

I pull out my credit card and toss it at the bartender first. "I can buy my own drinks. Thanks." I grasp the glass and take a longer drink than intended, but this guy frustrates me so much I can't speak. "Look, Brian. I'm here. That's what you wanted."

Brian cocks an eye at me as he looks me up and down. "Uh, huh. You're right. I was hoping the pretty lady I invited to a bar would wear her Saturday morning cleaning clothes. My wish has come true." His dancing eyes tell the story of what he thinks of me as he takes a swig of his beer.

"I'm leaving. This was a huge mistake." I take another sip and turn to go. Brian puts his hand on my arm, but I shake it off.

"Meggin, *Meg,* I'm sorry. I was teasing." He sighs. "Please stay. I'm not a bad guy. At least finish your drink. I forget you're not Tori." He picks up my wine glass and waves it in the air.

"Who's Tori?"

Brian grunts in disgust. "She was my on-air partner in Tucson. Let's just say we had a competitive relationship at work."

Something tells me Brian and Tori had more than a work relationship.

"I'll talk to Jerry. I promise. Do what I said. Find something you are passionate about, whatever story it is that you want to tell. Figure out the details. Do the legwork. You're a damn good reporter—too good to be stuck doing shitty pieces about car accidents and chocolate milk."

It's the first time Brian Welter has seemed remotely human since I've met him. I look at his face as it softens to something that resembles a real smile. "Then why are *you* here if you're covering the same kinds of stories?"

Brian snorts and almost drops his beer. "Honey, I have bigger dreams. I've been biding my time in medium markets around the US. I'm not about to let this opportunity in a large market go to waste. I'm shooting for the anchor job. Steve Larders is grayer than a koala bear in a gum tree. He's old news. I'm new news and Jerry knows it. I'm biding my time. You'll see." He grins, the perfect teeth his parents likely paid for in his pre-adolescence gleaming white.

"You're a cocky asshole, you know?" I see the twinkle in his eye as I set my empty glass on the bar.

"I know, but you don't get what you want in this business without knowing what you want and having the confidence to get it. Think about what I said." He throws a five on the bar as a tip and walks back to his friends. "Be careful walking to the train."

I watch Brian walk away and wonder if I'll ever have the confidence to pursue my bigger dreams. And if I really have to be a jerk to achieve them.

Chapter 5

Dad and I are driving behind Rick and Lara who are driving the U-Haul truck that is loaded with his and Mom's things, at least what is left of them. Turns out Dad wasn't as attached to his things as I first thought. He'd asked Lara and me to make drop-offs at our neighborhood charities. He'd been rebuffed at the charity nearest him for making too many deliveries. Everyone's junk is not, as thought, someone else's treasure. Saying goodbye to his old house, the house he built his life in with Mom, Lara, and me, was the only time I saw Dad choke up. He didn't say anything. He didn't have to. I got it. We *all* got it.

Dad drives, something he's always been confident doing. I hate the traffic on Interstate 80/94 through Indiana between Illinois and Michigan. It's a nightmare no matter what time of day you go, but it's especially busy in the summer months when Chicagoland residents travel to their summer homes in Michigan. Dad seems to read my mind. "I'm becoming a real FIP now," he says, smiling.

"Dad! Don't say that!" I first heard the derogatory nickname Michiganders have coined *not Friendly Illinois People* when I visited my college roommate in St. Joseph, Michigan. She was a transplant from Illinois, so she laughed it off and said the influx of summer residents helped the economy, but she said that locals took the invasion of strangers as nothing short of an intrusion of their very existence. "Does Blue Lake have many transplants or summer visitors, Dad?" I don't know anything about the small town Dad has chosen to call home other than its location: about an hour from Lake Michigan and that he's not chosen a beach town. He should at least have chosen a beach town—cute shops, good food, sand between your toes, warm breezes off the lake in the summer—that kind of thing. I don't understand anything about this move. Why would you want to live in the middle of nowhere when you know no one and have no family nearby?

Dad doesn't answer right away. He takes a deep breath, seeming lost in thought before he speaks, "I've heard the town is growing."

"That's good."

"You've lived in Chicagoland your whole life. I can't imagine not having a Starbucks or at least a decent local coffeehouse to go to every morning. What about a gym? You like working out. Do they have stuff like gyms and shops?" I realize the question seems silly, but I've never lived in a small town. I don't know what's in store for my dad.

This time he answers right away, more animated than I've seen him this whole trip. "Oh, yes! They have a great gym. Lots to do there. I'll be fine, Meg."

"But why this town? Why Blue Lake, Michigan?"

Dad rests his hand on my knee. *"Cooperative Community,"* Dad says.

"Cooperative—what?"

"It's a funny story, actually. It turns out there's already a little town north of here called Blue Lake. So, the founders of *this* Blue Lake solved the problem by making it a cooperative community."

"What the hell does that even mean?" I ask, more frustrated than ever.

"Trust me. This is going to be what's best for the family." He stifles a cough as he clears his throat.

I roll my eyes out of his view and look out the window. How on earth could our widowed father moving three hours *away* from his children and grandchildren be a *good* thing?

We hug the coast of Lake Michigan for the first sixty miles over the Indiana border into Michigan. I've been in some of these towns. Dad and Mom would take us to the beaches *across the pond* as Dad liked to say. He claimed the beaches on the Michigan side of the lake were nicer—cleaner. I didn't disagree that they were cleaner, but I much preferred going with my friends to Oak Street Beach in Chicago, playing volleyball, and ogling the guys throwing footballs in the water. That's where I'd met my first serious boyfriend Alex. He didn't have much to offer the world except for being something pleasant to look at. I didn't care when I was 21, but when I was 23 and nothing had changed, I knew it was time to leave the relationship. It was the easiest breakup known to man. Just a *hey, I'm taking my toothbrush and pajamas back to my place* kind of comment followed by a *yeah, sounds good, Meg.*

I dated a little here and there after that relationship, but no one interested me enough to seek more than a second date—until I met Will which lasted less than a year. And that relationship ended two and a half years ago. Watching Lara get married and have one kid, then two, then three, and I think maybe being alone is my destiny. And I'm okay with that.

39

We drive away from the Michigan coast past Holland, the namesake of the European country, and an adorable town known for its tulips in the spring. This is new territory, lots of land, some with cows and some with fruit trees, a random field with unknown crops. Michigan has sandy soil unlike the deep black, rich soil in downstate Illinois. "Are we almost there, Dad?" He is smiling, and I can't complain about that. Seeing him happy is what this is all about, right?

"Just about, Meg." He points straight ahead. "You see that tall building in the distance up there?"

I squint through the sun and make out a building that seems out of place in this barren landscape, maybe six or seven stories high. "What's *that* doing there?"

"Ha! Ha! That is the Blue Lake Hub, a building built to accommodate the new residents in Blue Lake. That is my new home."

"You're leaving Chicago for only God knows why and moving to a tiny town in the middle of nowhere to live in a *skyscraper?*"

"That is exactly what I am doing. Brilliant, huh? Can't you see how splendid this will be?"

"Can't say that I do, Dad."

He ignores my reply as we drive closer to town. I have to give it to this middle of nowhere town when it comes to hospitality. There are billboards—actual billboards in empty fields—popping up to announce the impending arrival into Blue Lake, Michigan. *Welcome to Blue Lake Cooperative Community. Home of Hope. Best Choice You've Ever Made.* The bright red backgrounds stand out against the quiet landscape. Is this why Dad has sounded like a walking billboard? Because he has been reciting *actual billboards?*

Dad pulls up to the front of Blue Lake Hub, parking behind the U-Haul that Rick has driven into a no parking zone. Blue Lake Hub looks like a building that has been pulled out of downtown Chicago and plopped into the middle of nowhere land. Floor-to-ceiling windows. Symmetrical balconies. A giant rectangle with no personality.

"I'll be right back. I need to tell Rick where to park and grab my keys."

I watch Dad walk away. He seems so vibrant and full of life, more so than I've seen him since Mom died. He'd been her caretaker for the ten months she'd suffered from the cancer, her body wasting away with every breath she took, fighting to the very end to hold on to that last breath. He deserves to be happy. I only wish he didn't think he'd have to move so far away from his family to find happiness.

A knock on the passenger window startles me. It's Lara. I lower the window. "Hey," I say. "Long drive, huh?"

"What the hell is he thinking?" Lara's face glows red. "What *is* this place? A skyscraper? A crap small town?"

I laugh. "You sound like a FIP," I say.

She wrinkles her nose. "What is that?"

"Never mind. I agree, Lara. I don't understand any of this. But you can't deny that Dad seems happy."

"He doesn't know what happy is anymore. He's all mixed up in his brain. This is insane!" She waves her arms around like *she's* the crazy person.

Everyone that passes on the sidewalk smiles at her. It's like they all nod their heads in a secret language they share. *We understand. We get it. This seems crazy. But you'll see.* I take a deep breath and try to clear my thoughts because they make no sense.

"Alright, girls…" Dad surprises us both. "We can unload the truck here. I'm going to park my car in the parking garage.

I grab my purse and close the car door behind me. Lara and I stand on the sidewalk together now while Rick pulls the U-Haul truck closer to the front door. A coffee shop across from the Blue Lake Hub is so busy a line forms outside the door. A steady stream of people passes on the sidewalk, some with blankets in their hands. Where are they going?

"This place is awesome!" says Rick when we are standing in the entryway of Dad's new condo—six floors up.

Lara and I shake our heads in disagreement. Nothing is awesome about this, but my brother-in-law couldn't read a mood if his life depended upon it.

"Thanks, Rick," says Dad as he deposits two more boxes in the corner of the living room by the large window that looks out over the town. He coughs to clear his throat. He seems out of breath. This move is too much for him. "I've been on a waiting list for three months for this place."

"Dad!" says Lara, her eyes nearly bulging from their sockets. "Three months? You've been planning to move *here* for three months?" She balls her fists in anger, but I know my older sister. She's going to cry. She reaches into her pocket and pulls out a tissue.

"I have, Lara. It's a popular place, but the top floor has the best views." We follow him to the sliding double doors on the other side of the living room. He glides the door open. We walk onto the balcony—room enough for the four of us and a couple of chairs and a grill—bigger than most Chicago high rise balconies. "Look at this magnificent town." He waves his arms over the air as if anointing the town below. "You can see the lake over there." He points in the direction of the path where I'd seen people walking on the sidewalk earlier.

"What lake, Dad?" asks Rick. "Lake Michigan is at least an hour away and in the other direction."

"Not Lake Michigan, of course. That's Blue Lake, the namesake of this community."

"There's not much to it," says Rick, ever the king of obviousness.

Dad chuckles, but his eyes twinkle. "I think it's the most beautiful lake I've ever seen. You can make it across in about a half hour."

"What's on the other side?" I ask.

"How do you get across?" asks Lara. So many questions.

"There are a few shops, the library, and a little restaurant across the lake, though you could get there by driving, too. This is a boat town," Dad says. "But quiet boats." He gazes off in the distance toward the lake as if he's already there floating by himself surrounded by nothing but quiet.

"You mean canoes or kayaks or paddle boats?" Rick can't stop snickering until Lara elbows him in the side.

"That's exactly what I mean. Doesn't that sound lovely?"

I put my arm around Dad. "It sounds like you think it's lovely, so that's all that matters." But I don't mean it. And I don't understand it. And I don't like it.

Chapter 6

It feels good to be back in the city after an emotional weekend of moving Dad to Michigan. It's a busy morning, too. A hold-up on the Metra line into the western suburbs has turned into a hostage situation. This is a street reporter's dream. *Drama. Unknowns. Emotions.* Of course, I'm not sadistic. I don't want anyone to be harmed. But the lead up to the safe releases makes for interesting news.

Brian isn't the newbie-in-training anymore. He's just the newbie. After the chocolate milk story and one other on a State Street mugging, Jerry started assigning Brian his own stories. Part of me was jealous as I'd had to shadow a senior reporter for months before being set free on my own stories. Jessalyn Bowers was that reporter. She hadn't made my life easy. Despite having grown up in and around Chicago, she treated me like I didn't know north from south. Arrogant and condescending, she'd tested my patience and my resolve to continue as a journalist. When she was promoted to evening anchor, and my only contact with her had to be feigned niceties over on-air banter, I was relieved to say the least.

I know Brian comes from a medium-sized market in Tucson, but he doesn't know Chicago, not like someone born and raised here. Chicago is in my *blood*. You report stories differently when it's your people. Plus, I don't need a Google map at my fingertips to get to my stories.

"Put the phone away," I say to Brian as I brush past him to grab my jacket. The freeze of winter is fading, but it's a cool spring afternoon. "I know where we're going."

This is a big story with lots of moving pieces. Brian and I haven't spent any time together since the night at Henry's when he tried to give me advice as if he knows so much more than I do about how to move up the ladder in a news station. Even if he does, it doesn't matter. I've been here longer. Seniority has to count for something, *no?* Jerry will see that eventually. But right now we need to get to the Ravenswood Station.

Tom takes the driver's seat while our newest camera operator Kelsey takes the passenger seat. She's learned on the job quickly though Tom is a great teacher. Plus, she has a killer laugh that makes every situation less tense. Brian and I sit in the back seat. "What's your angle" Brian asks as he pulls out his iPad.

"Angle? Are we in journalist class today, Brian?" I tighten my hair tie that pulls my ponytail a bit higher. I've been told I have nice cheekbones that look good on tv. I wonder if Brian's ever been given facial structure advice for television. Such a double standard.

"Play nice, Meg."

At least he's stopped calling me Meggin. "I'll try to talk to police on the scene. I have a lot of contacts on the force. You want to tackle the families on scene with loved ones on the train?" I ask, grabbing my old-fashioned but ever practical notepad and pen out of my bag.

Brian doesn't answer right away. When I turn to look at him, he's staring at me, his deep green eyes boring a hole above my nose. "Stop staring at me. What? Did I not rub in my foundation evenly?" I rub at my cheeks.

Brian smacks himself in the forehead and smirks. "Sorry. I'm just amazed how you can't see the obvious when it's glaring at you."

"The obvious?" I can see the stopped train in the distance as we get closer to the scene of the hostage situation.

"You're a storyteller, Meg. People don't want to hear from stuffy policemen who can't tell us much anyway. Interview the families. Tell their stories."

"But I have the police contacts. They won't..."

He stops me from talking with a wave of his hand in the air. He holds up his news channel badge. "I have *this*. They'll talk. Plus, I'm charming." He winks at me.

I wonder if this is some kind of trick, some way to scoop a story out from under me, but I don't have much time to decide as Tom is parking the van in the last tight spot left on the side of the road. "Fine," I say, opening the van door. "I'll look for family members. But treat the police with respect. Pay a little compliment if you can. They appreciate that."

"Do you think I'm new to this?" he says before breezing past me on the sidewalk. Kelsey races to keep up with him, clutching tightly to her camera. She's no complainer, though, and almost as good of a camera operator as Tom—*almost*.

A group of people stand huddled together against the crisp spring afternoon under a large sycamore tree that overhangs the sidewalk. I walk toward them when one of the people, a young woman with streaks of dried tears down her face, sees me. She stands up straighter, dabs at her cheeks, and meets me on the sidewalk. "Are you with the news?" she asks.

Tom stands behind me, camera in hand, so she knows the answer, but I'm not rude. "Yes, I'm Meg Popkin with WDOU news of Chicago. Are you a friend or relative of anyone on the train right now?" I ask, ready to pull my microphone out.

"Yes, my sister is on that train. She takes it every day to her job in the city. She was on her way back to Evanston."

"What is your sister's name?" I hold my pen over a blank page of my notebook. "And yours?"

"My sister is Annie. I'm Lizzie Ere. That's Annie's last name, too." She glances at the train and squeezes her eyes shut tightly before opening them again, clearly overwhelmed by the situation unfolding.

"May I ask you a few questions on camera?"

"Yes, I want to talk. I want everyone to know that this was going to happen—my sister—she knew something bad was going to happen, but the city didn't stop it." Her voice rises as she speaks.

"What did she mean by that?"

"Gangs. There have been gangs of kids riding the Metra, more and more. They usually just say some nasty stuff, sometimes reach out and touch someone, make them

50

uncomfortable. And no one's done a damn thing to stop it."

"So, you are saying that threats of violence have been escalating?" I ask.

"Yes, that's exactly what I'm saying. And now Annie is on that train with those criminals demanding only God knows what." She pauses, not feeling so empowered by the camera anymore, instead the thought of losing her sister becoming too real.

I put my hand gently on her arm and motion for Tom to put down the camera. "It's okay. I know you are scared. I really hope your sister is okay, Lizzie."

She nods and straightens her shoulders again, a momentary lapse in the reality of emotions. "Thank you."

She walks back to her family on the sidewalk, and I look for someone else to interview.

Editing runs the story with the police interviews front and center, giving the facts, the purpose of news, after all. I don't blame them though I'd fought for at least some of my interview with Lizzie to make it into the story. I'm satisfied. Brian's satisfied. He got the lead in the story, but I got *the story,* the heart.

"Nice work out there today," says Jerry as he passes my cubicle.

"Thanks, Jerry." As he walks away, I take a deep breath before calling out. "Wait! Jerry…uh…can I talk to you about something?" I look at my co-workers nearby and add, "…in your office?"

"Sure. I've got some time. We can talk now."

I stand up, brushing the crumbs from my evening sandwich off of my skirt, and follow Jerry into his office.

"Have a seat." Jerry gestures to the large leather chair in front of his expansive marble desk that rumor says has been in this building since it was built in the early 1900s. The previous station manager allegedly rescued it from an old storage room on the 45th floor, covered in cobwebs so thick a spider king himself must have lived there, or so the story goes.

"Let's hear the pitch," says Jerry. He sits across from me leaning his elbows on the marble monstrosity.

"Well, I suppose it *is* a pitch." I take a deep breath. I'd been thinking about what Brian said: bring Jerry the story because he won't offer it to you. "I really enjoyed today, I mean, not the victims being held on the train, and thankfully they all got out safely, but you know I like…"

"You like covering *people's stories*, not only the story," Jerry says, interrupting me. "I get that, Meg, but you're the best fact finder we have in this department. I can't give you over to the fluff stories. We need you on the hard-hitting news."

I can feel my cheeks getting warm. "Stories of human experience aren't *fluff*, Jerry. If anything, people *need* other's people's stories right now. They need that connection. Our world is so messed up because we've been separated from each other. Human emotion and story are what binds us together as a society."

Jerry raises an eyebrow. "News stations aren't the place for human emotions. You know that. They are places of facts."

"Of course, we have to give the facts. But we can do that and still share the impact that the facts have upon the real people involved, too. I argue that we *should* be doing that."

"What do you propose?" he asks, leaning back and seeming to relax.

"Before Mom died two years ago, she spent the last week of her life in Pine Crest Hospice Center. They were newly opened at the time and exceptional in the way they approached the end of her life care. I'd like to do a story about what they do and the impact they make for families who have to go through the experience of losing a loved one this way." I don't take my eyes off of Jerry while I make my pitch. "I'm confident I can tell this story—no, *should* tell this story."

"And why are you pitching this story now? Why not pitch it two years ago?"

I was ready for this question. I knew it was coming. "Because time softens experience, I guess. I needed time. And, well, now there's another reporter I know you trust to take the lead on some of the stories you'd assign me. Brian can fill in for me." I can't believe I've said it aloud. But it's true. Brian is abrasive and crass at times, but he's a good reporter.

"You know, some would think you're throwing in the towel. Giving up your place in this station because you're intimidated by another good reporter."

I can't shake my head *no* more profusely. "That's bullshit. You know that. I'm not intimidated by anyone. I believe in this story. I believe in telling *people's* stories. Let me tell them…please."

Jerry doesn't hesitate. "Fine. Tell the story. Tell the *stories* as you say. But it better be a damn good one because I need Brian *and you*. Until I'm given a better budget those other reporters out there," Jerry says, nodding at the station room, "are only subpar. I need you. And I need Brian."

"You won't be disappointed, Jerry. Thank you."

I wait until I'm in the bathroom stall at the end of the hall before I let myself breathe deeply. I close my eyes, rest my hand on my stomach, and take slow, deep breaths. This assignment isn't just about telling others' stories. I was reminded again of the fragility of life this morning when I interviewed those families being fearful for their loved ones' lives. And with a place like Pine Crest, death doesn't have to suck so bad. At least it can suck with dignity.

Chapter 7

"Need a ride?" Brian's too perky voice surprises me. There's no old cigarette smell today.

"Cutting back?" I ask as I swivel in my chair to face him. He's wearing a navy blue ¾ zip up shirt with the station call letters.

"Huh?" he asks, furrowing his eyebrows.

"You don't smell," I say and smile at the absurdity of my declaration.

"Well, most young women I've encountered have found that to be a good trait." He smiles.

"I *mean,* you don't smell like cigarettes."

He takes a step back, a hint of blush rising up his neck. I can't help but find joy in his uncomfortableness. "I...I'm trying to cut back."

"Good. It's an ugly habit."

"Anyway, I wondered if you needed a ride out to Pine Crest. Jerry told me about your story, and I'm heading downtown to do a story about a protest near the Art Museum. Tom and I can give you a lift, pick you up when you're done if you want." He looks over my head as he talks. Is he nervous?

56

"Uh…sure, I guess. I was going to walk, but I'll take a ride. But don't wait for me. I'll walk back to the station when I'm done."

"Sounds good. Meg, for what it's worth I think a hospice story is cool."

"I don't know if that's the word I'd use after my family's experience but thanks."

"Okay. I'll let Tom know you're riding with us. We're leaving in ten."

"I'll be ready, but you might want to change."

Brian looks down at his shirt. He smiles. "Don't worry. I'll be fashion model ready in five. See you soon."

I watch Brian walk down the aisle between the cubicles, waving at various staff members along his path. I still don't like him, but I don't hate him anymore. And Jessalyn Bowers surely doesn't hate him. It takes a full thirty seconds after he's passed her by for her to stop staring at his ass.

The entrance to Pine Crest Hospice Center is highlighted by three large flower pots, each trying to outdo the next with the beautiful arrangements of brightly colored combinations of flowers. My favorite is the one with pink geraniums, Mom's favorite, too.

I give my name and show my station identification. It's only a formality as Hannah knows me well, but she's training a new young woman at the front desk. When Mom was here for the last week of her life, I spent every moment away from the station with her. Lara left the kids with Rick and practically moved in while Dad *did* move in—if you call sleeping on a sofa in her room every night and only going home to shower moving in. Hannah greeted us with a tender smile every time we arrived, no matter what time of day. It's almost as if she lived here, too.

"Spencer is in the office. He's waiting for you, Meg. Do you…do you need a reminder…" Her face lights up like a gentle angel. It must be a job requirement.

"No. Thanks, Hannah. I remember the way."

She buzzes me into the main living area of the hospice center. A couple of family members sit in high-back flower-upholstered chairs talking quietly with each other. They look up at me with knowing looks, a fraternity of family you don't ever want to be a part of yet can't escape, preparing to say goodbye to a loved one.

I walk down a hall designed to be wide enough for wheelchairs though most patients here don't leave their beds. I knock on the last door on the right.

"Come in," says an enthusiastic voice from the other side of the door. It sounds out of place to hear someone so cheery. But to those familiar with a place like Pine Crest, a spot where people go to die, it's not at all unusual to hear joyful voices if the hospice is doing its job well.

"Hello, Spencer," I say, extending my hand. "It's nice to see you again—under different circumstances."

Spencer takes my hand. His grip is as I'd expect it to be for a young man, strong and confident. He meets me at my eye level—short with an athletic build—with a radiant joy that lights up the room. "Hello, Meg. I'm so glad you called. Pine Crest welcomes the opportunity to spread the news of our program. The more people we can reach the better. It's quite an honor to be featured by a station like WDOU. Have a seat." He gestures in the direction of another flower-covered chair, this one with a low back.

"Thanks," I say. "I intend to do just that, tell the people of Chicagoland not only about this wonderful facility but what hospice programs, in general, can do for families whose loved ones are dealing with end-of-life care."

"Great! Then tell me how I can help." He rests his elbows on the simple oak desk in front of him.

I pepper Spencer with a list of questions. "What brought you to this line of work? How does the program work here at Pine Crest? How does a family qualify? What services do you offer?"

When I am satisfied with the foundation of the information I've been given about the workings of a hospice program—the focus on providing comfort and dignity in a person's final days with things like pain relief and meeting psychological needs—I want to go deeper. "Tell me the stories of some of your patients."

"Stories?"

"Yes, I want to know about some of the families that have used the services of Pine Crest, besides our family, of course. I want to know what the process was like for them and how their experiences of using an in-patient hospice program helped.

Spencer is silent for a moment before speaking. "Every family is different, Meg. You know that. Plus, I don't feel right divulging that information. However, I do understand why that knowledge is important to telling the full story of Pine Crest, or of any hospice program, really. I will reach out to a few people that had family members here recently. If they are willing to talk with you, can I give them your contact information?"

"Absolutely. Yes, that would be great. Thank you, Spencer, for your time and for the work you do here." I stand to leave.

"Meg, wait. I..." Spencer runs his hand through his thick hair.

"What is it, Spencer?"

"I don't know if I should tell you this or not, but..."

I sit back down in my chair, my heart racing. "What is it?"

"It's about your mom."

"Okay." My mouth feels dry.

"When your mother was here, there was a moment...there was a moment when your dad had gone home for a quick bit. I like to visit the patients at least once a day, though as you well know, they rarely know I am there."

I grip the armrests of my chair.

"Anyway, I stepped into your mother's room. She was sleeping. I was there only a minute or two, checked that she was comfortable and such, and I started to leave. That's when I heard something."

I suck in a deep breath.

"Did you say something, Julie? I asked her as I moved closer to the bed. She reached for me, and I gave her my hand."

"Extra ice," she said.

Then she let go of my hand and closed her eyes again. I assured her I'd get her extra ice though I have no idea if she heard me or what that even meant as she clearly wasn't drinking on her own at that point.

I hold back the tears that pool in my eyes. I attempt a smile before I speak. "She always asked the waiters for extra ice." It comes out like a whisper, but Spencer hears me.

"I love that," he says. "And I hope she got her extra ice when she got to whatever the next destination on this journey is. I'm sorry I didn't tell you sooner. I honestly didn't think it meant anything. This just goes to show I still have a bit to learn on the job. There are more things to learn about these patients, even when they don't have much more living to do."

"Thank you, Spencer. And I have no doubt that Mom got her extra ice. She was *very* persuasive."

He chuckles. "That's great to hear. She was a special lady. And I'll reach out to a few possible contacts today. I think you'll hear from them soon."

"I appreciate your time."

Spencer walks me to the front door. I wave goodbye to Hannah.

It's not until I have walked a block away from Pine Crest and am headed back to the station that I let the tears flow.

Chapter 8

More contacts than I have room for in my story answer my questions about their loved ones and their experiences at Pine Crest. Spencer was right, and I am also glad that he insisted that I hear the stories from *them*, not him. They are not his stories, after all. There is the family who took their terminally ill daughter to Pine Crest so she could watch the birds at the bird feeders out of her big window, the wife who took her husband to Pine Crest because she could no longer care for him at home, and they let her crawl into bed with him every night and cuddle close to him while he slept in his medically induced state of peace. So many stories, so sad yet so hauntingly beautiful at the same time.

"A couple of us are heading to Henry's after work for nachos and beer…and pinot," I hear from behind my desk along with a school-boy giggle. "Want to come?"

I turn around, snapped back to reality. "Hey, Brian. I'm driving to Michigan tonight to spend the weekend with my dad. But thanks. And…" I can't believe I'm about to say this, but it's the truth. "And thanks for putting in a good word for my stories with Jerry. I'm working on an important story, and I think you may be part of the reason I'm getting to tell it."

"Don't sell yourself short, Meggi—*Meg*. Jerry didn't need much convincing from me. He knows you're talented. Everyone knows you're talented." His smile is somehow nicer when he doesn't act like an ass. "Plus, I'm getting to fill in for Steve when he's on vacation next week. Moving on up!" He points to the ceiling.

I shake my head. "Well, I guess we are both getting want we want," I say.

Brian stares at me but not in a creepy way, more contemplative. "Maybe so," he says. "Though we always want more, right? It's human nature."

"I suppose." I shut down my computer, throw my notebooks into my bag, and pull out my train clothes to head home for the evening.

Brian puts his hand on my arm. "Don't do that," he says, pointing at my clothes. "I'll take you home. You have a long drive ahead of you and don't need to be riding that disgusting train."

I cock my head at Brian trying to read his motives. "I thought you were going to Henry's," I say.

He throws up his hand. "Changed my mind," he says. "I remembered that CNN is running a special on the fashions of the 90s tonight that I do not want to miss!" His eyes twinkle, as does a right dimple I'd never noticed before.

"Uh-huh. Sure, Brian." I glance at the time on my Apple Watch. I want to say *no,* but I do have a long drive tonight. I would have driven to the station, but I need to take Linda to my neighbor's to cat sit before leaving for Michigan. Her niece is visiting for the weekend and wants to have Linda stay at her place. I'm not so sure Linda is going to like being smothered by a little girl. "Okay, that would be really helpful, actually. Thanks."

Just then Jessalyn walks by. She's changed into a low-cut, thin blouse with tight jeans, and heels. I never did understand the jeans and heels fashion trend. Perhaps that look is featured on Brian's 90s special tonight. "I'll see you at Henry's," Jessalyn says to Brian as she squeezes his arm.

"Not tonight, Jessa. Have fun."

She looks at me and back again at Brian. "Hmm…that's a disappointment. Don't let Meg bring you down. She's got a knack for that. Catch you on Monday."

As she walks away there's an extra swing in her hips. It makes me want to puke, but Brian seems amused.

"Look, you can go to Henry's. I'm a big girl and quite capable of taking the train."

"No way. It's on my way home. I'll just grab my things."

Brian drives an Audi which is not a surprise. Only the color surprises me. Silver seems subdued. I'd have expected a bright red or shiny blue.

"Are you hungry?" Brian asks as he glances over at me in the passenger seat.

"Not if this is what you're offering," I say, pointing to an old McDonald's bag on the car floor at my feet.

"Oh, yeah, that was breakfast. It's my one indulgence of the day."

Watching Mr. Confident be embarrassed is entertaining. "I thought your original plan was getting nachos and beer tonight?"

"Ohh, yeah...that was a..."

"Lie?" I fill in the blank.

"Just an excuse to spend more time with you," he says so softly I almost didn't hear him.

Now it's my time to feel embarrassed.

But Brian makes the moment pass by swinging back to Mr. Confident mode. "At least let me grab you a Starbucks. You need to stay awake while you drive." He pulls the car into the Starbucks parking lot and drive thru lane.

I don't protest. I don't want any more weird Brian confessions. "Thanks. I'll take a tall espresso, please."

"Plan to stay up all night?" he asks, raising an eyebrow with his dimple dancing on his face.

I shrug my shoulders. "It's a long drive." I pull a ten dollar bill out of my wallet, but he waves it off.

"My treat."

We don't talk much as he drives to my apartment. It's been a nice little home in Brookfield, a suburb outside of the Chicago city limits. The zoo in Brookfield is my quiet place. I turn my head in the direction of the zoo entrance as Brian follows the instructions to my apartment. Nothing gives me more peace than sitting in a crowd full of people at a packed dolphin show.

"Which way, Meg?"

"Oh, sorry. I was at a dolphin show."

"Excuse…"

I giggle. "I mean, I was thinking about the zoo—Brookfield Zoo. It's right over there." I point out of my window.

"That's cool. Is it a big zoo?"

"Bigger than big. It's one of the best zoos in the whole country. It's awesome."

"We don't have great zoos in Tucson."

"Too hot," we both say at the same time.

We laugh. "But there's a great museum outside of Tucson that has lots of animals, too."

"Are they stuffed?" I ask.

"No, not all. Well, *some* animals might be, but there are also live animals like mountain lions and hawks and javelinas."

"*Javelinas?* Turn right at the next stoplight."

"Yeah, they're kind of like wild pigs. I was jogging once in the middle of a neighborhood when a javelina ran out from between two houses and scared the crap out of me. I about peed my pants."

"Now *that* is something I'd have liked to see," I say. "The wet pants, I mean. That's hilarious. Hey! You missed the turn."

"Shit, sorry."

"It's okay. Take your next right."

Brian pulls up to my three story walk up. I'm on the top floor which is a dream come true. There are no noisy neighbors stomping their feet at all hours of the day while I'm trying to rest or read another book I'd picked up while thrifting. "Thanks for the ride. I hope it didn't add too much time to your commute." I reach for the door handle.

"No, it's fine. I'm another thirty minutes east."

"*East?* That's back to the city," I say, looking at Brian incredulously.

"Yeah, do you really think *I'd* live in the suburbs?" He roars with laughter, his perfect teeth on full display.

"Then why did you give me a ride? My apartment is completely out of your way."

Brian shrugs his shoulders and stares out his side window. "Maybe I thought Starbucks was better in the suburbs."

"You're crazy," I say, opening the car door. "Thanks for the ride."

"Meg, wait." I turn back toward him. Now he's looking right at me, but I'm not uncomfortable. "I…I hope you have a good visit with your dad. And drive safely."

I smile. "Thanks, Brian. See you on Monday." I shut the car door and unlock the front door of my building. Brian doesn't drive away until I'm safely inside.

Chapter 9

It's after 2:00 a.m. when I pull into the parking garage in Blue Lake. I take out my cellphone to talk to Dad as I make my way to the elevator though I don't feel unsafe, the opposite feeling I'd have in a Chicago parking garage at 2:00 a.m., for sure. I have to change elevators in the lobby. It's well lit, and even though it's an hour later in Michigan's eastern time zone, there are groups of people lounging in oversized brightly colored chairs. What looks like a heated game of euchre is happening at a table in front of a speaker that is piping out a catchy jazz tune. Looks like a perfect Friday night to me.

"Meg!" Dad pulls me in with a bear hug when I walk into his condo. He feels thinner, perhaps as a result of all the walking he says he's been doing.

"There's a bit of a party going on in the lobby," I say as I hang up my jacket in the front hallway closet.

"Oh, yes. That party goes on seven nights a week. I've won a few pennies down there myself." He laughs as he pours me a glass of water, extra ice.

I take the glass gratefully. "I imagine everyone trips over themselves to be your partner, Dad." I sit on a stool across from him as he looks out the floor-to-ceiling windows behind me.

"They do. I'm popular, at least when it comes to euchre. "Will you look at that view, Meg.?"

I follow his gaze back to the window. The lake is illuminated by surrounding lights, the water shimmering like tiny crystals bouncing about. "It's nice. Peaceful."

"Well, at least this time of night it's peaceful." He chuckles.

I roll my eyes. "I don't imagine there's much of a big city vibe going on in Blue Lake during the day."

"Not a big city vibe. That's true. But it's a bustling town, lots to do."

I don't see how that's possible, but I don't want to burst his bubble. Plus, I'm exhausted. "Can we talk more in the morning? I'm beat."

"Absolutely! It's way past my bedtime. The guest room is all set up for you. Help yourself to the towels under the sink in the bathroom. I'll see you in the morning, at least later in the morning. I hope you brought your walking shoes."

"I don't have any shoes that don't walk, so I think I'll be just fine. Goodnight, Dad." I kiss him on the cheek and head to bed.

It's odd staying with Dad and not sleeping in the bedroom I'd grown up in. So much has changed. I always thought Dad would stay in that house until he died, too. I never wanted a new place—a place like Blue Lake—to be a part of my memories of my dad. I toss and turn as I think about these things. Plus, Dad's intermittent coughing *and* snoring is really loud, even through the wall. Eventually exhaustion wins out.

Dad is dressed and waiting for me when I walk into the kitchen. "Good morning! Ready for breakfast?"

"Sure. I don't turn down food," I say, reaching for the coffee cup he has sitting on the island.

"Finish your coffee and we'll head to Rosie's."

"Rosie's? We're not eating here?" I ask, looking for a pantry with cereal or a banana.

His eyes light up with amusement. "No way. Life's too short for boring breakfast. Everyone eats at Rosie's."

"Everyone?"

"Darn near everyone. We have reservations at 9:45."

"Reservations for *breakfast?*" What is this place?

"Trust me. You'll understand. You'll feel it, too."

Feel it? Why is Dad acting so weird?

The late spring air is invigorating, the perfect mix of briskness mixed with the warmth of the sunshine on your face. Dad has given me a jacket to wear even though I'd brought my own. *It's warmer than what you have, Meg. Just take it.* It still feels nice to be parented when you're all grown up—sometimes.

Rosie's is only two blocks away, and small-town blocks are shorter than city blocks, but it takes us fifteen minutes to get there. Everyone knows everyone. *Hello, Paul. How are you today, Paul? Did you catch the sunrise, Paul? Is this one of your pretty daughters you were telling us about, Paul?* I don't understand. Is this what *all* small towns are like? Or is it my dad's chipper personality that brings out these questions?

Rosie's is hopping. Dad wasn't kidding. Every table is full, and the wait staff are twisting their bodies to squeeze between patrons as they bustle about taking orders and filling drinks. I expect to see mostly people of retirement age, like Dad, but I don't. There is a mix—people in their

90s down to people in their 20s. Though weighted toward the older demographic, the younger population is taking up more of the seats than I'd expect in a town this size. I wonder if they are people, like me, visiting a parent or grandparent.

"Your table's ready, Paul," says a young woman with very short black hair, so short it reminds me of Mom's hair when she started to lose it during her first round of chemo. But she's smiling so large her whole face looks radiant. It's nearly contagious.

"You're popular in Blue Lake," I say after ordering a short stack of pancakes from the young lady named Mellie.

Dad takes a long drink of his coffee, cream with added sugar. "I'm not special here, Meg. You see, *everyone* is special."

"I don't understand." I look carefully at all of the people around me, most laughing and smiling with overfilled plates.

"I know you don't. Someday you will. Trust me when I say I'm happy here. It's the best thing—for all of us."

I don't have time to argue because Mellie has returned with my short stack of pancakes that is anything but short. "Thanks, Mellie. It looks delicious. Have you been in Blue Lake long?"

She looks from me to Dad and back again. "Not long." And then she walks away but not before depositing another grin.

I just shrug my shoulders and turn my attention back to the giant plate of food that is sitting in front of me. "They sure like their food in this town."

"Yes, they do," Dad agrees as he digs into his oversized omelette.

After breakfast I can barely move. Rosie's food is no joke. It's the kind of place where you feel guilty leaving food uneaten on your plate because it tastes so damn good. My stomach is so full that all I want to do is lie down and let digestion do its thing. But Dad's going on and on about not wasting time. *Things to do, Meg. Things to do.*

So, I pop a Tums and follow Dad to the lake, the infamous Blue Lake from which the town has received its name. I guess I won't be using my car this weekend. We walk another two blocks to the lake. We aren't alone,

77

though. The sidewalk fills up as we get closer to the people coming from all sides of Blue Lake to converge upon this main walkway.

"Head that way," he says, pointing to a sidewalk that leads to what looks like a large shed near the water.

Ken's Kayaks the sign says. "Are we taking a boat?" Sure, I'd been to the beach with Dad before, usually on family vacation to Florida when I was little, the Gulf Coast being our favorite spot, especially shell hunting on Sanibel Island. But I'd never seen my dad on a boat, unless you count the boats on the *It's a Small World* ride at Disney World.

"We are taking a boat across Blue Lake. The library's across the lake. You'll love it, Meg."

I'm touched that Dad has heard my musings about choosing a different career path, but can't we drive to the library? Seeing how giddy my father has become, though, allows me to bury my frustration.

"Two kayaks," says Dad as we reach the counter. Apparently, a lot of people are boating across the lake. I wonder if they are all headed to the library, too. And what do you do if you capsize, and your library books go for a swim?

"Sure thing, Paul," says the man I assume to be Ken. He's young, maybe even still a teen. I wonder why he's not in school. And does he also know everyone in Blue Lake by name?

Ken hands me a blue paddle. Dad gets a red one. I look around. The people waiting for their kayaks at the shore are all holding red paddles, too. *Am I special?* or do I scream *tourist*, and we get the blue paddles?

A young woman, perhaps even younger than Ken, pulls returning kayaks into shore. An elderly couple get out of the boats with her help, thank her, and hand over their red paddles. The older man grabs his wife's hand, and she pulls him up the small hill back to the sidewalk. "This was the time, Bob. This was the time," she says over and over. Bob shakes his head in agreement though I wonder what he thinks he's agreeing to.

Dad leaves shore first. I have to paddle faster to keep up. Yes, I definitely think that his weight loss is due to his activity level increasing two-fold, three-fold, five-fold. Who knows what else he does when I am not here? I can't deny the beauty of the lake, though. It's nearly clear. I can see lake plants growing on the bottom with large fish weaving their way in and out between their leaves. Even the fish seem happy in Blue Lake.

There are more people on the other side of Blue Lake waiting to help people out of their kayaks than into them. Dad lets me glide in first. A young woman stifles a cough in her shoulder before reaching her hand out to me. A man with patchy tufts of curly hair helps Dad.

"Good to see you, Paul," says the man.

"Looking good, Charlie. Kate, Charlie, this is my daughter Meg." I swear they take a simultaneous glance at my blue paddle before breaking out in wide grins.

"Nice to have you visit Blue Lake," says the girl named Kate. "Your dad is quite a guy."

Dad's face lights up with the compliment. "It's easy to be a good guy when you are surrounded by so many good people," Dad says, returning the compliment.

"What brings you to this side of the lake today?" asks Charlie.

"Meg here is a book enthusiast, a not-so-secret hoarder, in fact. We are heading to the library."

"It's a hoarder's dream, a jewel in Blue Lake, for sure," says Charlie.

"Have fun," Kate and Charlie say as we begin our walk to the library.

Everyone in this town is so friendly. It's not natural. Is it just because it's a small town? Is that the way small town people act? Surely not all of the time?

The library is situated on prime lake-front property. Dozens of outdoor couches and chairs sit on a deck that overlooks the lake. I have to admit the thought of grabbing an iced tea and sitting on the deck with this view and the perfect book sounds like an ideal way to spend the afternoon.

I follow Dad inside. As soon as we enter, a woman about my Dad's age hands me a blue cloth bag. Dad pulls an identical bag from his backpack, but it's red. "What are these for?" I ask.

A bandage covers the woman's cheek but not her huge smile. "For the books, of course. You can put your books in the bag until you are ready to leave. It makes your experience more comfortable. Every visitor is given a bag." She glances at Dad. "And repeat visitors are encouraged to bring their bags back. Thank you, Paul."

"You're welcome, Gwen. Come along, Meg. You have to see the mystery books' room. It's outstanding."

I follow Dad through the stacks to the mystery room, most definitely a mystery as to its location to me as the giant stacks of books create a maze that I'm not sure I could navigate alone without several repeat visits.

"This place is huge," I say. "It's almost as big as the Harold Washington Library in the city."

"I knew you would love it."

I read the labels at the end of each bookshelf. The self-help section alone must be 500 books. Who needs that much help? At last, we come to the infamous mystery book room. In here, the bookshelves line the four walls, floor to ceiling, with those only-seen-in-the-movie ladders that slide along the shelves if a patron wants a book too high to reach. In the middle of the room are high-backed, plush chairs with ottomans and side tables. A coffee machine sits plugged in on a marble-topped bar with a plate of individually wrapped cookies.

"I think I could live here," I say.

"Not yet, Meg." He stares off into space toward the W-Z books.

"I didn't mean *move* here."

"Oh, of course not. No..no…that's not what I meant, of course." He reaches for the coffee pot. "Care for a cup?"

"Sure."

"Pick out a couple of comfy chairs. Let's catch up about work," he says.

I glance around. The one person who was in the room when we arrived left after greeting Dad. I swear she stared at me too long before leaving. People judge for the oddest reasons. What's wrong with me now? I check my socks to make sure that they match.

"I've been doing all the talking today," says Dad. He hands me my coffee cup. "Your turn. I saw your story online about the hostage situation at the train. It had over 50,000 views."

"Ha, my wanna-be tech savvy father. I'm just relieved that things ended peacefully. Could have been much worse."

"Yes. I don't miss the threat of violence here."

"Nowadays, Dad, violence can happen anywhere, sadly."

He shakes his head emphatically. "No, not here. Not in Blue Lake."

"Okay, Dad. I'm not here to argue."

"Of course not. Tell me about your personal life—doing anything for fun?"

I grimace. "I know what you're doing. Stop it. I'm quite happy by myself. And to answer your questions, I go to the gym for fun, take an occasional run along Lake Shore Drive on the weekends, and am finishing my seventh Jodi Picoult novel."

"Sounds riveting," he says, his eyes twinkling.

"It *is* riveting. Life is exciting. Living the dream." I pick up a small pillow and chuck it at Dad's lap.

He catches it and flings it back to me. "Seriously, though, I want you to be happy."

"Are *you* happy, Dad?" I ask, looking around the expansive room full of mysteries and realize I still can't solve the mystery as to why my dad decided to move his entire life three hours away from his family.

He leans closer to me and puts a hand on my knee. "Meg, I'm happier than I've been since Mom died. Things are getting better, in every way."

I study my dad. "I'm glad. I really am." I still don't understand, but I'm grateful. Life is, after all, one big mystery.

We wave *goodbye* to Gwen when we leave the library. Dad checked out a Kristin Hannah novel for me using his library card, so my blue bag is useful after all.

"Let's bike back," if you don't mind. "I don't want to get our books wet." He taps his red bag which is full to the brim.

"Don't tell me this tiny town has a rentable bike system like downtown Chicago?"

"Nah, it's not like Chicago. Here the bicycles are free." He grins.

"Of course they are." I roll my eyes.

We walk down a small sidewalk from the deck of the library. Dad speaks with everyone who crosses his path. How could so many people live here? There aren't *that* many streets. The skyscraper condo building makes more and more sense.

"You take that one," says Dad, pointing to a shiny, blue bicycle with a large basket. I put my bag inside and ring the little bell for fun. It makes me happy and takes me back to the memory of a vacation in the Outer Banks of North Carolina when Dad, Mom, Lara, and I rented bicycles with bells that we rode along the boardwalk. We saw four dolphins, a little family like ours. It's a nice memory.

Dad climbs onto a rusty red bicycle that seems to have seen better days.

"Why don't you take this bike, Dad?" I ask, pointing to another blue bicycle that looks pristine.

"Nah, this is fine. It's just well-loved."

He starts pedaling before I can argue. As we round the lake, I try to slow down my breathing and take in the sights. It really is a beautiful place. Spring is my favorite time of year. The tulips are blooming as are the flowering pear trees. The lilac bushes along our route fill the street with a magical smell that could lift anyone out of the mopes as Dad would call Lara's and my teenage moods. And in the distance stands Dad's condo building, like a compass orienting yourself in town.

"Watch the speedbump," says Dad as we approach a bump in the road.

The reasoning for the speedbump is curious as there really aren't many cars in Blue Lake, but then I notice a large stream of people diverting to the left down a street marked simply as *Hope*.

"Where are those people going, Dad?" I ask as we pedal around the speed bump and past the entrance to Hope Street.

"Oh, nowhere special. Keep pedaling. I want to make it home in time for *Wheel of Fortune*. Almost there, Meg!"

I don't believe him, of course. Dad has monologues about every part of this town. Why the secret about Hope Street?

After dinner at home (and *Wheel of Fortune*), Dad and I take large glasses of wine to the balcony overlooking our view of Blue Lake. Dad steadies himself against the wall before crossing the threshold to the balcony, perhaps a sign that he's doing *too* much in his new favorite town. I sit down in a wicker rocking chair and take a long sip before pulling a light blanket around my lap, the spring night creating a nip in the air.

"So, tell me about work." Dad sets down his glass and crosses his legs. He looks like a mixture between a banker and a college professor. "I believe we never finished that conversation at the library."

"Uh-huh. Well, I'm working on a new story—kind of a feature."

87

He sits up straighter. "That's awesome, Meg. What's the topic?"

I clear my throat. "I'm writing a story for the Thursday night news feature section about Pine Crest Hospice Center."

Dad widens his eyes in surprise but nods as if understanding. "That's interesting. Do you think that's wise?"

"Why wouldn't it be wise?"

"Pine Crest holds painful memories for our family. Plus...," he hesitates, "...maybe it gives families false hope."

"Dad! What on earth on you talking about? *False hope?* Pine Crest didn't give us false hope, not me at least. We knew Mom was going to die. She was going to die with peace and without pain. How is that *false hope?*"

"That's all true, of course. I mean...I mean...I think..."

"Dad! Say what you're thinking."

"I think there are other ways to live than giving in to death. And places like Pine Crest give people hope that their family member is dying with grace when there may be another way...another way to *live.*"

I shake my head back and forth in quick succession. "What are you talking about? How could there be another way to live when you're going to die? Do you not think that Mom was going to die? That we made a mistake taking her to Pine Crest?" I stare at the man before me, seeming a stranger.

"I...I don't know. Maybe if she'd known...never mind, Meg. Don't mind me. Just the ramblings of an old man." He stands up and pats my knee like I was a little girl. "I'm tired. I'm going to bed. Get some sleep, too. You have that long drive back tomorrow." He winks at me. "Plus, my girl's got a feature story to write."

I watch Dad walk back into the condo, again reaching for the wall to steady himself, and I wonder what this seemingly idyllic town is doing to him.

Chapter 10

I shut the lights off in the back office at the station where I've just completed a Zoom interview with a woman whose husband had died peacefully at Pine Crest two months ago. I didn't realize how emotional I'd be hearing the woman's experiences. The man, Grayson, had only been thirty-eight when his kidneys started to shut down. Kidney failure was his *death sentence,* as his wife Jami called it, but she said that Pine Crest had been their life preserver, maybe not extending Grayson's days but holding onto the comfort that the last days would be peaceful and without pain. Their five-year-old daughter had even been able to visit her dad and play at his bedside, memories that Jami said she will be forever grateful to Pine Crest for.

I need to call Spencer again to schedule another interview, this time with the camera. The story is due in a week which includes the tapings. There is so much to do. I gather my notes and laptop before shutting off the light. I push open the door into the hallway.

"Ouch!" I hear before I realize I've slammed the door into the unfortunate staff member who passes by.

"Ouch!" he says again, his hand flying up to his nose.

"Oh my gosh! I am so sorry. I...*Brian?*"

"Hi, Meg." Blood is spreading through his fingers as they squeeze his nose.

"Oh no! I'm so...here, take this." I reach into my pocket, pull out a wad of tissues, and hand them to him.

"Are these clean or dirty?" he asks in a muffled voice like a McDonald's employee through a drive thru box.

"Clean! I'm not that sinister! But by the way you look, I think even dirty tissues would be helpful. Come on. Follow me." I set down my stuff, grab for his free hand, and pull him toward the staff bathrooms.

"Really, Meg? The women's bathroom?"

"Anyone in here? Hello?" I ask, propping the door open with the trash can.

"Come here."

Brian follows.

"Sit down," I say, pointing to an old striped couch that looks straight out of a college house, beer stains included.

"You have a couch in your bathroom?"

I roll my eyes. "Yeah, but don't get any ideas. I've tried taking a nap. It is *not* recommended. Here." I hold out a wet paper towel, taking the bloody wad of tissues with a dry towel and throwing them away. Something tells me this wasn't the way my on-board employee training taught me to dispose of bloodborne pathogens, but I'll throw the trash down the chute later, an advantage to being in a 48-story building. "Pinch your nose and lean forward." I hand him another wet towel. "Let me see."

He slowly removes the paper towel while looking away.

"Are you afraid of blood?" I ask, trying not to giggle.

"Who loves blood? Man, you are ruthless today."

"I'm sorry. Really, Brian. I'm so sorry."

"What were you doing in that office anyway?" he asks, dabbing at the last remains of blood droplets.

"I was having a Zoom interview with a woman whose husband was under hospice care at Pine Crest."

"That explains why you were distracted."

"Yeah, kind of brought up some—*stuff*."

"Want to talk about it?" Brian's voice softens.

A brief moment of silence passes between us before there is a knock at the bathroom door. "Everything okay in here?" It's Kelsey.

"Meg's trying to kill me," yells Brian. "Save me, Kelsey!"

Her laughter echoes through the bathroom as she sees Brian's bloodied nose.

And just like that, the moment is gone.

After taping a quick story with Tom at the courthouse about a local chef's preliminary hearing for embezzlement in a popular steakhouse restaurant, we drive to Pine Crest.

"What do you have in mind for today?" asks Tom as he wipes his glasses on his jeans, a light drizzle falling outside.

"Spencer told me there is a family he wants me to meet. A young man whose sister is in Pine Crest's care is willing to be interviewed to share his experiences with the hospice program. I think we will use the common room for the taping." I pull down the visor in the van to check my hair. Drizzle and my hair don't play nicely together. I try to push down the frizz that's forming.

"My wife spits on her hands," says Tom.

"What?"

"When her hair gets frizzy. She spits on her hands to smooth her hair. It helps. You should try it."

I laugh. "I'll take that under advisement, but I have some product I think I'll use when I get to Pine Crest."

"Suit yourself."

Hannah greets us and points me toward the bathroom. After I've made myself at least presentable, I take a deep breath. I place a hand over my heart and wait until the beats slow. Tom is talking with Spencer when I walk into the common room. Sometimes I think Tom should have been the reporter instead of me. He's a people person.

"Hello, Meg. Nice to see you again. How is your dad?"

"He's great," I say. "Well, he thinks he's great. He moved to Michigan, kind of living a retired life over there. It's not the most common choice for location—a very odd, little town, in fact—but he's good."

"Blue Lake?" Spencer asks.

"How did you…?"

At the same time I'm waiting for Spencer to answer, a young man walks out of a patient room and toward us. "This is the man I told you about," whispers Spencer. He walks slowly, eyes downcast as he moves closer to us. His youth gives way to a heaviness that he carries in his drooping shoulders.

"Hi, Darrel," he says. "How is Robin?"

"She's comfortable," he says. "Mom and Dad will be here soon to sit with her. Thanks."

I have a sudden urge to give this stranger a hug. I understand the pain. I understand the uncertainty.

"Hello, Mr. Manning," I say. "My name is Meg Popkin." I reach out my hand.

He shakes it. "Nice to meet you, Ms. Popkin. But please call me Darrel. Mr. Manning is my father. And he's an old man."

"Likewise. Call me Meg."

We all smile, a nice tension reliever. "If you don't mind, I'd like to ask a few questions about your experiences with hospice care, specifically at Pine Crest. I'm doing a story for WDOU on the value of end of care treatment that hospice programs can offer."

"Yes, Spencer told me. I'd be happy to answer your questions."

Happy is such an odd choice of words, but I appreciate his willingness to talk to me. "I know this is hard, Darrel. I need to ask you the questions on camera, but I'm going to ask you why you are here, I mean, why your family member is here, what lead you to make this choice for her, and what the experience has been like for you. Are you comfortable with that?" It's not at all how I handle most interviews. I don't give questions away first. It's better to get the answers naturally, get the authentic answers and reactions—usually. But this story is different. I feel like I owe it to Darrel to prepare him before Tom starts the camera.

"Of course. Thanks. Do I…Do I look okay?" He runs a hand through his thick blonde hair and wipes imaginary crumbs from his shirt.

"You look great," I say. I touch his hand gently. "I promise."

"Okay, I'm ready then."

Darrel answers all of my questions with confidence and ease. Robin, his younger sister by four and a half years, had been in a boating accident. She suffered a lot, physically and mentally. Three years after the accident she started having mini strokes. Doctors didn't know if it was related to her accident though they couldn't rule it out. Two weeks ago, Robin suffered a serious stroke and has not regained consciousness. Her doctors have assured the family that there is nothing more they can do. And at 39, Robin is going to lose her life. The last option the family had was to let her die with dignity and grace and free from as much pain as possible. The staff at Pine Crest has been wonderful, as they had been for our family. Anyone who wants to sit with Robin is welcome to be here, at any hour of the day. And she is given a cocktail of drugs—under her doctor's care—that keeps her comfortable until her body shuts down. Darrel's experience has mimicked mine, but hearing about a young woman dying gives a whole other *f you* to grief.

"Thank you," I say when Tom turns off the camera. "Robin is lucky to have such a caring brother."

"I haven't done anything for her that she wouldn't have done for me. Is it okay if I go now? Mom and Dad just walked in the common room a minute ago, and I think I should be with everyone."

"Of course. Thanks again." I shake Darrel's hand before he walks away to Robin's room. He embraces an older man and woman, his parents. The three of them walk into Robin's room together.

Spencer taps me on the shoulder. I jump, lost in my thoughts. "Can I show you something, Meg?" he asks.

"Sure." Tom and I follow Spencer down a hallway that exits the back of the common room. He pushes a set of buttons on a keypad at the back door and pushes the door open onto a large courtyard surrounded by a wrought iron fence. Well-pruned trees and fountains with running water adorn the landscape with intersecting sidewalks for countless ways to walk around the courtyard. In the middle of one of these paths, Spencer stops.

He squats down and pats the dirt. "Do you see these tulips?" he asks, spreading his hands above the wide array of beautifully colored flowers in nearly every color imaginable.

"They are gorgeous. I'm sure the families and staff enjoy seeing them."

Spencer bends down to pull a couple of stray weeds. "Yes, of course. But do you know who planted these?"

I don't understand why that would matter, but I don't say anything.

"The patients, at least those patients strong enough when they arrive, plant a bulb. This is the patient's garden."

"That's nice," I say. Mom was nearly comatose when she arrived at Pine Crest, so she didn't plant a bulb, but it's nice to imagine those that do.

Tom records shots of the tulip garden. It will make a nice addition to my piece. I ask Spencer a few questions on tape before we leave. Spencer opens the gate to the courtyard that leads back to the parking lot when we are done. We say our *goodbyes,* but before I get more than a couple of steps outside the gate, I turn around. "Spencer, wait! I have one more question."

Spencer walks back to the gate. "Yes, Meg?"

"Sorry. Something is bothering me. You...you say that patients plant those bulbs?"

"Yes. They do a beautiful job." He looks admiringly at the flowers sprouting up in the courtyard.

"Yes, lovely," I agree, "but why? I mean...why do they plant them knowing that more than likely they won't...they won't be here anymore—*alive*—when the bulbs bloom?" I whisper the end of my question as speaking it aloud is painful.

"Meg," Spencer's voice softens. "These tulip bulbs represent *life*. They are planted when the patients still have life, of course, but even if their life is no longer here—in the physical sense—when the flowers come up out of the ground, it's still a reflection of the continuance of life—and hope that life continues. Because it does. It has to."

I nod my head, lost in thought. Neither of us speaks for a moment. "Thanks again, Spencer. Thanks for what you do."

"It's my pleasure, Meg."

Chapter 11

The buzzer from the outside of my building rings when I've just finished dinner—microwave chicken nuggets and green beans—gourmet meal for a single almost thirty-year-old female. I check the screen on my end. I can't believe who I am seeing outside my building on this drizzly night though I'd be shocked on a sunny evening as well to see Brian on the other end of my camera.

I push the call button. *"Brian?"*

"Hey, Meg. Sorry to drop by unexpected. I was in the neighborhood. Really, I was. I have a buddy that I play basketball with on Sunday nights, and his car broke down. I gave him a ride. I was just stopping by to say…well, I'm not sure why I'm…Can I come up?"

"Okay. I'm the top floor unit." I push the buzzer to let Brian in. Then I scan my living room and fly into a flurry of cleaning. I throw away the rest of my nuggets, stacking my plate in the sink along with yesterday's dishes. I pick up a jacket, a cardigan, a stack of magazines, some books, and a pad of paper and throw them into my coat closet. I am folding a throw blanket when Brian knocks on the door. Linda jumps off the couch and runs to hide, not a huge fan of unexpected company, or of any company for that matter.

"Hi, Meg," he says. He's holding a bottle of wine. "I brought this." He holds up a bottle of pinot grigio.

"Thanks. Do you have random bottles of wine lying around in the back of your car when you give your friends unexpected rides home to the suburbs?" I arch an eyebrow and look at Brian skeptically. He is wearing jogging pants and a green hoodie. The green brings out the color of his eyes. I feel my cheeks getting warm as I linger too long.

"Well, um, the ride for my friend wasn't a lie, but I *did* stop at a liquor store to buy the wine." Brian smiles, a hint of guilt reddening his cheeks.

"Did you want a drink?" I ask, walking toward the kitchen. I run my fingers through my tangled hair. Why didn't I at least brush my hair?

"You know it!" he says, following me.

I grab two wine glasses from the kitchen cabinet and search through a drawer for my wine opener.

"Need some help with those dishes?" He points to the stack sitting in my sink with caked on remnants of last night's pasta sauce.

"Not funny. Perhaps if you're expecting a clean sink, the next time you decide to visit someone on a Sunday night you should give a call first."

"Fair point. Plus, you have expert taste in chicken nugget brands." He points to the trash can that is overflowing.

"You're a chicken nugget connoisseur?" I ask sarcastically.

"The real question, Meg, is what type of sauce do you dip those fine nuggets in?"

"Well," I say as I hand a glass of pinot to Brian and take my own back into the living room. "I prefer barbeque, but a good honey mustard is nice, too."

"That's my girl—I mean, I agree. Sorry. Yes, good answer." He perches on the arm of my couch while I sit in an easy chair across from him.

"Why are you here, Brian?"

"I told you."

"But why—*really*?"

Brian sighs. "You said you were finishing your Pine Crest story this weekend. I knew it must be hard with your personal experience and all. I...I was just checking on you."

"I hardly think that the *great* Brian Welter has time to think about his lowly co-workers."

"Another fair point. I'm not always a dick. Sometimes I'm genuine."

"And how might one know if you're being genuine?"

"Spend enough time with me, and you'll figure it out."

"Hmm…"

"So, how is your story coming along?" He takes a long swig of wine and sets it on my coffee table, using the only coaster I own.

I exhale slowly and sink back into my chair. "It's been tough. But I'm pleased with how the story ended up. All I have to do is film my part at the station and edit."

"That's great. Is it still airing on Thursday?"

"It is."

"I can't wait to see it. You're living your dream, Meg."

I nearly spit my wine out of my mouth. "One feature story hardly makes a dream. Just because Jerry let me do this story doesn't mean he will let me do another.

Plus, I've got so many daily assignments there's hardly any time to fit this story in."

"Yeah, but that bank robbery was pretty cool, huh?" He laughs and takes another long drink of wine.

"Strange choice of adjectives. How are you liking Chicago?"

Brian pauses before answering. "I like it. Chicago is a vibrant city, always something happening, lots to do and lots of news-worthy events, of course. The weather sucks."

I gasp. "The weather is *awesome* right now!"

"A high of 55 degrees is *not* awesome." Brian sneezes.

"Bless you. Okay, Mr. Arizona. Just remember that in the middle of summer when it's 85 degrees and you can actually *breathe* outside unlike in Tucson."

"That part I am looking forward to, no doubt."

I smile, realizing it's nice to have another living being in my apartment to talk to. As if on cue, Linda jumps onto the couch, crawling out from her hiding spot under Brian's chair.

"Holy crap!" Brian yells. He jumps up quickly which make Linda jump, and she goes running off to hide again. "You have a cat?"

"Uh, I had a cat until you scared the living daylights out of her.

"Me? She scared me. You never told me you had a cat."

"And you never told me you were coming over," I snap back.

"I'm...I'm sorry. It's just that I'm allergic. *Really* allergic." Brian starts scratching his neck where red hives have started to form. He looks around, panicking, taking short breaths. He sneezes again. "I have an EpiPen in the car. I have to go!" He bumps into the coffee table, knocking over his empty wine glass.

"No. Wait! I have an EpiPen."

"You have an EpiPen?"

"I have an EpiPen! I'm allergic to peanuts. Hang on!" I run to my room and rummage through my nightstand. Linda stares at me from under the bed. I grab the EpiPen and close the bedroom door behind me.

"Here!" I thrust the EpiPen into Brian's hands. He drops his drawers with the other hand and jabs the EpiPen into his thigh. Brian's breathing relaxes, a truly magical medicine. I've used it myself when I ate a peanut butter cookie at a birthday party by accident.

Brian takes a slow deep breath. Then his eyes get big as he looks down at his bare, pasty white legs and navy blue briefs. "Meg, please don't, oh man, please don't…" He quickly pulls up his pants.

I can't help but laugh. "If I'd known it was this easy to get rid of my co-worker, I'd have invited you over earlier."

He throws a pillow at my head. "You are terrible. *Terrible.* I think I'd better go."

"Brian, I'm sorry. I had no idea Linda would try to kill you." I shrug my shoulders.

"I should have known you were trouble when you nearly broke my nose at the office."

"Oh, man, I *am* trouble!"

"You are full of surprises. Thanks for the EpiPen. I really mean it. You saved my…"

I put my hand on his chest. "Stop! I didn't save your life. I gave you medicine."

"Please keep your cat at home," says Brian. "I'll see you tomorrow. Can we keep this quiet?"

"But this might be the kind of story Jerry is looking to fill at the end of the news segment tomorrow night!" I throw back my head in glee.

Brian puts one finger to my lips. "Quiet, please." And he kisses me.

Chapter 12

I've managed to avoid Brian most of the week. When Jerry asked for reporters to cover a rally for gun safety rights, I'd deleted the email as soon as I saw Brian's reply in the affirmative. Instead, I took a story down at city hall about a tax hike for garbage pick-up, and I *hate* going to city hall. I'm not ready to talk to him about what happened the other night at my place. It was so unexpected and uncalled for, and yet I can't stop thinking about it. *The kiss. And Brian.*

"How's your hospice care story coming along, Meg?" asks Jerry as he slings his arm casually over the top of my cubicle.

I pivot my chair around to face him. "It's good. I need to do a bit more editing, but it will be ready for the segment at the end of tomorrow night's 6:00 news," I say.

"Good. That's good. And how was *city hall?*" His eyes dance with merriment because he knows. *No one* likes city hall.

"Fantastic. Things down there are awesome. No double-speak at all." I laugh.

109

"Seriously, Meg, I'm surprised that you didn't jump on the gun safety rally story. Seems right up your alley for your sudden interest in the emotional stories."

I sigh. "It's not a *sudden* interest, Jerry. I've just been here long enough that I finally feel like I can choose the stories that interest me."

"Like a garbage tax hike?" He has now folded his arms across his chest.

"I'm already busy enough with the hospice feature. I just chose something easier."

"Uh-huh," says Jerry before turning to walk away. "You've never taken the easy way out," I hear him saying as he's walking toward his office.

I take a call from Lara while I am eating my lunch at a picnic table on the roof of the Arbor Building where WDOU is located. It's a beautiful day, 65 degrees, light breeze blowing on my face. It's days like this I wish for a minor accident or fender bender story so I can be outside working. Nothing bad, of course. I'm not inhuman.

"Do you have time to talk?" Lara asks as I take a bite of my ham and cheese sandwich. Singledom's finest lunch.

"Yeah, it's good. What's up?"

"Dad," says Lara.

I straighten up and put down my sandwich. "What's the matter?" I can't get the words out fast enough.

"Oh, nothing. He's fine. I mean he's not fine. He's acting…"

"Dammit, Lara! You scared the crap out of me. You can't do that!" Kelsey looks up at me from a nearby table as I'm yelling at my sister. I wave.

"I'm sorry, Meg. I'm sorry. I'm…I'm just so flustered. Dad is acting so weird."

"I agree. What happened this weekend?"

Lara sighs so loudly I have to take the phone away from my ear.

"Rick and I took the boys to Blue Lake. There are so many people there, Meg. It's like a suburb, but it doesn't *feel* like a suburb. Does that make sense?"

"Totally," I say as I recall the streams of people that walked everywhere, particularly toward the lake.

"Anyway, the boys were crazy about Dad's condo. I had a heart attack every time Nolan wandered onto that balcony. I couldn't sit still. But that's not why I'm upset." She takes another deep breath. "Dad took us on a picnic at a little park down by Blue Lake. He *insisted* that the boys carry these blue buckets—you know, those sand toys with attached shovels. Nolan and Owen kept dropping theirs, so I put them in my Meijer grocery bag I had taken out of the trunk when I knew we'd be walking everywhere. Dad wouldn't have it. He said the boys *had* to carry the buckets themselves. And he gave Rick this crazy ugly sun hat to wear. He said he'd bought it special for him so Rick couldn't tell him no."

"What color was the hat?" I ask, sitting up straighter and brushing the crumbs from my sandwich off my yellow, flower-printed blouse.

"What?" Lara sounds as irritated as Jerry when a story's late coming out of editing.

"What color was the hat?" I ask again.

"Rick's hat?"

"Lara, listen to me. *What color was the hat that Dad gave Rick to wear?*"

"It was blue, Meg. The damn hat was blue. Why?"

"And did he give *you* anything?"

"No, Dad didn't give me anything but a headache. Well, actually he gave me a jacket because it was a bit chilly."

"And what color was the jacket, Lara?" I can't believe I didn't see it before.

"It was too big for me, of course. It was just a light blue wind breaker," she says. The lightbulb flips on. "Oh crap! Meg, everything was a shade of blue. What is going on?" she asks. "Nolan, not now," I can hear her saying to Nolan who is whining for his mommy. "Meg, what is going on?" she repeats.

"I don't know. I really don't. But I got a blue paddle for our boat trip and a blue plate at dinner and a blue bag at the library."

"Wait! The stupid town is called Blue Lake! That's all. Everything's fine. They like the color blue."

"Lara, what about Dad, though? What color did he use or have or whatever when you were out together?"

Lara pauses. I can hear Nolan and Owen playing in the background, Blake at school. "Red," she whispers. "Dad had a red jacket and a red bag. And his coffee cup at the restaurant downstairs was red."

"Shit," I say. "The same thing happened when I was there."

"Meg, what is going on in Blue Lake?"

"I have no idea, Lara. But I'm going to find out."

Chapter 13

My inbox is full when I check my station email. Spencer, Hannah, Darrel, Jami, all complimenting the hospice story that ran last night as the Thursday feature story. But it wasn't only emails from people who'd been part of the story. Strangers reached out to thank me for what I'd written, telling me their stories: a woman who'd watched her mother suffer and decline at home with no outside help or support because she didn't know that there *could* be help or the man who said his fears about his terminal illness were lessened when he found out about Pine Crest and learned there were options for helping his transition to be pain free and easier for his family, too.

"It's your lucky day," I hear Kelsey say as she laughs heartily behind me in my cubicle.

How could such a strong sound come from such a small woman? But she always makes me joyful. I turn around. "What do you mea..." Kelsey is holding a bouquet of lilies and daisies in a vase that is tied with a yellow polka dotted bow. "Are those for me?"

"Of course they are." She thrusts the vase into my hands. "And they come with a note, too, but I didn't peek."

She laughs again. "But I wanted to. Tell me who they're from, Meg!"

I set the flowers on my desk and open the envelope. The card on the inside is simple.

Good things happen when you pursue your dreams and stand up for yourself. Well done.

"Well...who sent them?" She jumps up and down like a giddy schoolgirl, and others are staring, especially Jessalyn from her office. Anchors get offices, and hers, with large windows, looks directly at my cubicle.

"The card isn't signed. But I think they are from my dad. He's been calling and texting since the story ran, telling me how many more views the story is getting on YouTube."

"Aww, that's cool, Meg. Your dad really loves you."

I smile and nod. "Yes, he does." *But he also confuses the hell out of me, too*, I want to say. But I don't.

"Meg, Brian!" I hear Jerry yelling as he runs toward my cubicle. Brian's desk is at the end of the hallway. "Police scanner says there's been a shooting outside the Chicagoland Science Museum. I've already got reporters covering a crash on I-90 and a pothole story downtown. I

115

need you guys to head out there. Tom should be back from lunch in a couple. I already texted him. Meet him out front in five."

I hate this part of my job. I'm a planner by nature, and the news industry thrives on the *breaking* part of a news story. I run to the bathroom to reapply my makeup. I pull a brush through my hair, put on my suit jacket, and push the elevator button just as I meet Brian there. He is straightening his tie and running his fingers through his hair. He looks rattled which is not normal. "Did Jerry catch you unexpectedly?" I ask as we walk onto the elevator.

"Yeah, no, I mean…I was in the middle of something. But it's all good." He takes a quick breath.

"Everything okay?"

"Yeah, yeah. Everything's fine."

We don't speak again until we are in the van with Tom. Brian doesn't even fight me for the front seat.

The Chicagoland Science Museum sits on an island of sorts, located between bustling Lake Shore Drive and Sixty-Seventh Street. It's the oldest museum in the city of Chicago and houses over 100,000 exhibits. Dad, Mom, Lara, and I spent many family excursions visiting the museum, so many so that my parents purchased memberships for a few years. But I haven't been back since Will and I broke up. We'd gone on a winter date that ended up in a huge fight in the train exhibit room. I don't even remember what we were arguing over, but I left him there and wandered over to the miniature castle room which always brought me peace. Tiny exquisitely decorated rooms adorn an enormous display in five different miniature castles with more details one can take in on one, two, or even three trips. Will swore like a soldier when he finally found me. I don't think Will had ever been to the miniature castle exhibit which was a big red flag.

Brian is out of the van as soon as Tom comes to a stop in the parking lot. "Brian, wait!" I yell as I race after him in my less-than-practical pumps. I can hear Tom running behind us, too.

Brian pushes his way through the crowd of reporters that are standing near the steps of the museum behind the police tape. There are dozens of police cars and ambulances at the site. This is more than a single shooting. This might be a mass casualty event. My heart sinks. Even one life is worth covering, but when that number is multiplied it agonizes the community and damages the soul of our great city. This is the worst part of my job.

"Excuse me. Sorry. Excuse," I say to the dirty looks I am getting from my competitor reporters. This kind of behavior is really frowned upon.

"Dammit, Meg. What the hell are you doing?" yells Ramona McClintock, a reporter at WECL whom I've just shoved into the camera guy in front of her.

"Sorry!" I yell rushing past, but I don't really mean it. Ramona is a bitch.

I reach out and grab Brian's jacket when he's finally stopped running, as close to the police line as possible, some would say even skirting their parameters. "Brian! Stop moving!" I pull him back from behind.

He snaps his head around and shouts at me. "Let me go, Meg! LET ME GO!"

I drop his jacket and stare at him. There's nothing more I can do. He's like a man possessed with an invisible, uncontrollable force. If that's what he wants, he can have this story. I don't want to be here anyway.

"What's wrong with Brian?" Tom whispers in my ear. "I've seen passion for a story, but this is a whole other level."

"Ego does things to people," I spit back, angry that I have to be *here* and that I have to be *here with Brian*.

"Are there victims?" Brian shouts.

Tom pulls his camera to his shoulder, Brian asking questions faster than he can get set up for the shot. "Are there victims?" he yells at the nearest police officer.

The police officer looks at Brian with no emotion, his training kicking in to be stoic in times of tragedy. No one should have to experience a shooting anywhere, let alone while visiting one of the best museums in the country.

When the police officer turns toward another reporter, Brian hops the police tape and runs in the direction of the museum steps. "Brian, stop!" Within seconds the very same policeman grabs Brian, puts him in handcuffs, and shoves him toward a police car. I don't think about what I'm doing next. "Wait! I climb over the same police tape and run after Brian and the police officer. "Wait! Wait! I'm Meg Popkin," I yell as I try to pull out my station credentials. "He's with us! Just an overzealous, egotistical reporter." Brian turns around and glares at me. That's when I see Officer Toby, my Dad's high school buddy, one of my many contacts in the force. "Toby! Mr. Welter is with me. I'm sorry. He's an ass," I say, sputtering my words, trying to diffuse a very tense situation. "Please let him go."

Officer Toby yells at the officer with Brian. "Let him go. But get him out of here, Meg," he says to me. "We have real problems here."

"Yes, I understand. I'm so sorry."

Brian is released from the handcuffs. But he can't stop himself from finding more trouble. "Are there casualties?" he asks right away.

"We will have a press conference as soon as we have more details. You can wait like everyone else." An ambulance runs its lights and races past us out of the parking lot. "Get out of here!" I know Officer Toby's *I mean it* voice. I've been on the receiving end before along with his daughter Mindy when we took his car for a joyride in eighth grade. Hearing it again gives me PTSD.

I tug on Brian's arm. "*Come on!*"

He tries to push me off. "But my sister and niece are in there!" he screams. The look of pain is visceral on his face.

I drop his arm. "Brian, I don't understand."

"Look, I'm sorry." Officer Toby's voice softens. "There's a family site set up at St. Luke's Church on

Ontario Street. I wish I could give you more information. Everyone is doing their best here."

Brian doesn't say another word as he walks away from the scene he's caused, now a part of the news story—five cameras directed right at him.

"Let us through. Excuse us. Please excuse us." I lead Brian through the crowd of reporters, Tom a step ahead of me making the path larger.

I open the door of the van, and Brian gets in while Tom stands guard at the back of the van. Brian drops his head into his hands and cries. I don't know what to do. There are no words for moments like this because moments like this shouldn't be happening in America. But I have to try. "Brian, I'm so sorry. I didn't know what you were doing—why you were doing it. And I—how is this possible that your sister and niece are inside a museum in Chicago when they live in Arizona?"

Brian clears his throat and looks up as if seeing me for the first time since we left the station. "Because they are visiting me on my niece's spring break," he whispers. "And because I told them to go to *this* museum on *this* day."

"I understand." I squeeze his arm while he hangs his head, the waiting overwhelming. What can you say? I'm not sure how much time passes, but the ding of a phone gets the attention of both of us.

Brian whips his phone out of his front pocket. His hand shakes.

I grab the phone before he drops it. And I read the text.

Safe. Hiding in the little castle room.

"Brian, they're safe." I hold the phone out so that he can read it.

Brian grabs me around the waist tightly and collapses against me. And we stay like that for a bit, Brian sitting on the back seat, me standing outside the open door, his head on my chest, my face buried on the top of his head.

And the only thing he says is, "What's a little castle room?"

Chapter 14

The last press conference of the day ends. This one was held at police headquarters instead of in front of the museum. The museum is closed, at least for now. We know many of the details though it doesn't hurt any less. At 3:37 p.m. a lone gunman entered the museum through the main entrance. His gun set off the metal detectors, but he reached its trigger before security guards reached him. Three people lost their lives, two museum employees and one guest. Then the gunman was tackled by brave patrons who held him down until police apprehended him. His only connection to the museum seems to have been as a patron who'd been arrested for walking out of the cafeteria without paying a month ago. None of it makes any sense.

I walk slowly back to the station van. Kelsey has been my camera operator today. Tom was overwhelmed this week. I don't blame him. Jerry sent him home early to be with his wife yesterday. And Brian has been put on leave for the rest of the week, possibly longer. He caused quite a commotion for the station when his handcuffing made him part of the story in local coverage. It wasn't a big part of the story at all, but some of our competitors liked to point out one of WDOU's reporters being put in handcuffs at the scene of a mass shooting. They made it out that Brian was trying to scoop a story the wrong way and interfering in police operations of a serious event. Jerry was pissed, like really angry. He doesn't like the station being embarrassed—his words—but when he learned why Brian acted like a fool, he put him on leave. Higher ups said he could come back in a couple of weeks, but he can't have any big stories again until some time passes. Brian's the source of office gossip, too. Jessalyn's been telling everyone that Brian's lost his mind, that he's become a loose cannon. She's just jealous he's getting so much attention. And Steve, who can't fathom the thought of being replaced despite having been at the station for twenty-five years, feels like he's won a sort of moral victory that will save his anchor job.

I'd texted with Brian a couple of times. His sister Natalie and his niece Gabby had flown back to Arizona a couple of days after the shooting. Thinking of Brian being alone in the city with only his new beer-drinking buddies for company has led me to a decision that I hope I don't regret and that I hope my dad doesn't make a bigger deal out of than it is. I'm going to ask Brian to go with me to Blue Lake. He needs a change of scenery. I need another reporter who can help me sniff out what's going on in that town. It makes the most sense though I don't really need that much convincing. I pull out my phone to text.

Hey. Have any plans this weekend?

Hi. Drinking beer. Lots of beer.

Not sure that's a great idea. But what do you think about drinking beer in Michigan?

Hadn't considered it.

I'm driving to Blue Lake on Saturday morning to see my dad. Weird stuff happening there. Could use a good reporter to help me figure it out.

And there will be beer?

At least pinot

Hmm…I need beer.

Fine. There will be beer.

Okay. I'll come.

I'll pick you up at 8:30 on Sat.

Like, A.M.?

Yep.

Damn. Okay.

Brian sends me his address, and I add the information to the contact for him on my phone. Linda jumps on my lap. She's good company. She listens to problems well and never talks back. But sometimes—just sometimes—I wish there was someone else sitting next to me listening to my problems. And it's okay if they answer back.

Chapter 15

It's the middle of May, and it is pouring down rain. Droplets so big hit my windshield as I'm driving into the city that I consider pulling over into the parking lot of a fast food restaurant, but I also don't like the idea of sitting alone in an unopened restaurant at too early Saturday morning, so I keep driving.

I pull into a no parking zone when I get to Brian's building and text him. A few minutes later he walks out of his building with a large black umbrella and the smile I'd missed. His blonde wispy hair is covered by a Chicago Cubs baseball hat, and a black windbreaker beads as the rain hits it.

"Hey!" he says, sliding into the passenger seat of my Honda Accord. "Good morning."

"You're more chipper than I thought you'd be after I texted with you the other night."

"I had an attitude adjustment since then—and three cups of coffee."

I smack my forehead. "Just great! Now we'll have to stop for pee breaks!"

His laughter fills the car. "Like we wouldn't have to stop for you!" He points to my travel mug.

"Fair," I say, laughing.

"Want me to drive?"

"Are you serious?"

"Yeah, I'm serious. It's crazy out here."

"And by asking, you do realize that you sound like a sexist asshole who thinks a woman can't handle driving in a rainstorm?"

Brian throws a hand up in defeat. "I was just trying to be nice. But forget it." He looks out the window, well, what he can see out of a rain-soaked window anyway.

I take a deep breath and exhale. "It's just that sometimes you come across really condescending. I'm sorry, but it's true—though you've gotten a lot better since the first day I met you."

"At the chocolate milk story?" he asks.

"Yep, that's the one."

"I wasn't being sexist or condescending or any of the other *wonderful* adjectives you have for me this fine Saturday morning on a trip *you* invited me on, I might add. I was figuring things out. It's hard being the new guy in a city I know nothing about. I was trying to project confidence. I guess it kind of came across as assholery."

"Is that even a word?"

"It is now," he says and chuckles. "Let me know if you need a break. It's a long drive."

"Thank you," I say, glancing at the not-so-smug-anymore reporter sitting next to me. "And thanks for telling me that."

"Telling you what?"

"About being vulnerable when you started."

Brian spits coffee out on his sleeve as he exhales loudly. "Let's not go *that far*, Meg!"

I laugh again.

The first half of the trip is a genial mix of office gossip, politics, and pop culture. I don't bring up the museum shooting. Brian doesn't either. I make sure to tell him what a bitch Jessalyn has been, though.

"So, you haven't told me yet. What's the big mystery I'm supposed to be unraveling?" Brian asks as he rests his arm on the steering wheel. I'd allowed him to drive after a quick potty stop at the gas station. Plus, the rain has stopped. The sun is trying very hard to make an appearance though I'm not so sure that it will today.

"Ugh, you're going to think I'm crazy."

"Don't worry about that, Meg. I already do."

I punch his shoulder and shake my head.

"Ouch! Being around you is dangerous."

I roll my eyes and ignore him. "Seriously…"

"I *am* being serious!"

"Stop it! Listen, are you going to help me or what?" I'm exasperated with this man.

"Fine, I'll stop. What's going on in Blue Lake?"

I sigh. "I wish I knew. For starters, Lara and I have no idea why he decided to move in the first place. He had a great house, grandkids, two daughters, a son-in-law, friends, a gym, plenty to do. It doesn't make sense."

"How long ago did your mom die?"

"A little over two years ago."

"Maybe your dad felt like he couldn't move forward in the house he'd shared with her, kind of like getting a fresh start. Could that be the reason?"

"I mean, I guess that can be some of it, but he didn't need to move to another state to live in a different house. And then there's all this weird stuff happening in Blue Lake." We pass the exit for Holland—not too much farther to go. "This town is in the middle of nowhere. Lake Michigan is here," I say, waving my arms over the direction of the lake. "It's awesome! It's gorgeous, in fact, especially on the Michigan side. And there are some decent-sized cities in Michigan, but Blue Lake is *not* one of them."

"There's something to be said about living in a small town, right?"

"That's just it! Blue Lake is teeming with people. Dad lives in a six-story building! There's not a single stoplight in town. There aren't even that many cars. People bike and walk and boat everywhere. And the sidewalks are *packed*. And everyone knows everyone..."

"That detail sounds like a small town."

"True, but this is the part that's going to make me sound crazy." I throw a hand over his mouth before he can answer back. "There's something weird about the colors blue and red."

"Huh? What? Meg, that *does* sound crazy."

"I know! But you'll see. I don't want to tell you more. I want you to use your reporter magic and see if you can figure it out. See if you can notice the oddities, too."

"I look forward to the challenge. It will be a nice change of scenery, for sure." He drops his voice as he stares straight ahead at the barren roads on which I direct him.

"Do you miss work?" I ask.

"Sure, I do. But I get it. I'm a liability to the station. Only time will make people forget the scene I caused."

"Everyone understands."

"If that were true, I wouldn't need a hiatus. I got an email the other day from some asshole who accused me of trying to make the story about me intentionally, like I crossed the police line to *become* the story. That's bullshit. I wasn't thinking about anything but my sister and my niece."

"People suck," I say.

"Yes, they do."

Chapter 16

"One more thing," I say before we walk into Dad's condo after being buzzed in by the doorman. I grab Brian's arm until he is facing me. "My dad will ask you a thousand questions. And he...uh...he falls hard for *anyone* I introduce him to. I've told him we are work partners, but I'm warning you."

Brian smirks. "Just work partners?" he asks, arching his eyebrow.

"Well, yeah, right?" Then the door opens, and we are smothered by my dad's embrace which makes me feel guilty that the main reason I am here right now is to snoop.

Dad gives Brian a tour of the condo while I go into the kitchen and help myself to three glasses, filling each with water and extra ice—for mom. It strikes me that I have no idea if Brian even likes ice in his water. All of the glasses in the cabinet are clear glass, nothing funny or odd or extra *colorful* there.

"Your views are outstanding here, Mr. Popkin. I can see why you chose this condo," says Brian who takes my glass-of-water offering and walks toward the balcony where Dad has already slid the doors open, letting the sunshine and the perfect warm breeze inside. There's no rain in Michigan today.

"Please call me Paul. Everyone does, especially friends of Meg's," he says, shooting me a not-at-all subtle glance.

"Yes, dad. *Friends.*" I take my glass and walk out to the balcony, too.

I point out places below that I have been with Dad: Rosie's for breakfast, the library, the kayak rental stand. I crane my neck to see the street which Dad had downplayed before. *Hope Street.* I really want to find out what's down there this weekend.

"I'd love to take Brian on a tour of Blue Lake. Plus, Meg, there are some things you haven't seen yet, believe it or not."

"I'm not sure I do. There isn't much land here, Dad."

"Perhaps that's true. The land that *is* here is well used and accounted for. Let's take a walk."

He grabs a ballcap. Then he grabs a second but seeing that Brian is already wearing his Chicago Cubs hat, he sets it down. He hands me a small box.

"What's this?" I ask.

Dad smiles. "Just a little something I found when thrifting. I thought you might like it." He shrugs his shoulders.

"But you already sent me that beautiful bouquet of flowers after my hospice story aired."

Dad wrinkles his forehead. "I didn't send you flowers."

"You didn't?" Now I am the one who is confused.

"They must have been from Pine Crest then, a thank you of sorts." I open the lid of the small box and find a crocheted bracelet inside with a single charm, a letter *M*. It looks like a wristband you'd wear to get into a music festival, like a small town's version of Lollapalooza. I slip it on my wrist.

"It's perfect," Dad beams. "Now let's take that walk!"

Brian follows Dad but not before giving me a goofy grin and pointing at the bracelet. He leans in close and whispers, "It's blue."

Our first stop is the hardware store, a block away from Rosie's Restaurant. Brian follows Dad to look for a toilet flapper because his master bath toilet has been running unnecessarily. I take the time to look around. I walk the aisles filled with everything normal as far as I can see. Nuts and bolts, nails, mousetraps, tools, garden supplies, paint. To be honest, this little hardware store rivals a big box store. Every square inch is filled from floor to ceiling. I guess when you live in the middle of nowhere you need a shop like this to get your home improvement needs filled.

A clerk behind the counter is talking with a customer about wood stain colors. The customer, a woman with short brown hair, has a thin summer tank on that barely covers something that protrudes from her waist. I'm wondering what it could be when the clerk starts coughing, so hard and deep that *my* chest starts hurting for him. He excuses himself and walks away from the counter, presumably to get a glass of water.

I walk over to the woman. "Excuse me, but is that guy, okay?" I point in his direction as he turns a corner a few aisles away.

The woman looks up startled. "Oh, Bill? You know he'll be fine, nothing a trip to the waterf…" A quick glance at me from top to bottom shuts her up the second her eyes land on my bracelet. "I mean, Bill, uh, yeah, he…he swallowed wrong."

It's kind of hard to swallow wrong when you're not drinking anything, but I don't respond as Dad and Brian join the checkout line. Another employee rings up Dad's purchase after the woman with the wood stain exits.

"Everything okay?" asks Brian, his hand on the small of my back.

I shake my head no as I say *yes* as Dad is only a step in front of us. Something is definitely not okay.

When we leave the hardware store, Dad links his arm through mine as we walk to Ken's Kayaks for another venture across Blue Lake. I match my steps to his, and I realize how nice it is to slow down a bit. I can't deny what a gorgeous town this is. As before, people fill the sidewalks, coming or going from around the lake. *Hello, Paul. Good to see you, Paul. Hello, family of Paul!*

"Dad, how well do you actually know these people?"

Dad smiles. "I know them pretty well, Meg. Only the finest live in Blue Lake. It's a special place."

I wish I could decipher the underlying meaning to that statement, but I can't. It's time to pick out a kayak.

"Hello, Paul!" says Ken as he reaches out to shake my dad's hand. "I see you have visitors again." He nods at Brian and me.

"It sure is a great day to be on the lake," says Brian. "Any chance we can get a double kayak?" he asks, winking at me.

I'm about to protest when I look at the kayaks and realize that the seats of the doubles tied to the dock are all red. *This* is the reason I brought Brian with me. "Yes! I think we'd like to take that kayak right there." I start walking in the direction of the double kayak.

But Ken springs into action, nearly jumping over the counter. "Sorry! Nope, that's not possible today. So sorry. But you and your husband are welcome to singles that you can tether together if you'd like."

I don't protest the use of *husband* because I'm concentrating on my debate skills from high school communication class. "We really want to experience the lake together. Plus, Brian's afraid of the water, and he'd feel better being close to me."

Brian clears his throat and rolls his eyes, but no one sees him but me. "She's right. I'm irrationally *terrified* of water. I've heard so many great things about Blue Lake, though, that I really want to get out there on the water. Can you tell me *why* we can't take a double kayak?"

Ken is flustered, his neck turning splotchy colors of red that rise up to his face.

"The email, Ken," says my dad. "That email you sent out about the holes in the base of the double kayaks…?"

"Oh, right!" Ken smacks himself in the head. The absurdity of this act makes me want to laugh, but I'm in reporter mode. "The manufacturer sent out a recall about this delivery of double kayaks having issues with tiny holes in the base of the kayaks that can lead to water filling the boat, and…"

"Wow! Quite a story, Ken! Then we'll take this one instead—to be safe," Brian yells as he grabs a double kayak that's just come in, the riders already making their way up the hill away from the lake. "It's obviously safe."

I follow quickly behind and don't tighten my life jacket until I am seated. Mission accomplished. Dad pats Ken on the arm, a sign of defeat, before he gets into a kayak also marked with a red seat.

"Nice work," I say to Brian who sits in the front of the boat as I steer us to the other side of the lake.

"You're right, Meg."

"About what? Your irrational fear of water?" I can't contain my happiness right now.

He splashes his paddle backwards, and water gets my shirt wet. "Ha! No, seriously! There is definitely something weird going on here. We have to get across the lake before your dad, see what happens when we show up with our kayaks."

"I think you're right, of course, but Dad didn't give you anything weird to wear and carry before we left like he did me." I roll my bracelet through my fingers which itches my wrist like crazy.

"He didn't have to."

"I don't understand."

Brian points to his Chicago Cubs hat. "Cubbie blue they call it, right? My hat is already blue—lucky, I guess."

"Damn, you're right."

"Hey, Meg! Hold up! You're paddling too fast," says my dad who is trying with all of his strength to catch us.

I feel badly, but I can't let him reach us, so I pretend that I can't hear him. Charlie, the man I'd met the last time I was here, is now bald, his tufts of hair shaved away. He stares for a second as if trying to place me. I don't fill in the blanks, and I hold my hand over my bracelet. Charlie holds a hand out for Brian, who has removed his hat, after he tethers our boat. Brian does the same for me as I step across the top of the kayak.

"I didn't know we had new residents in Blue Lake. I must have missed the email. It's my pleasure to meet you." He slaps Brian on the back and pulls me in for an unexpected hug. "Have you visited the waterfalls yet?" he asks.

A loud thud causes all of us to turn toward the lake. Dad has crashed his kayak into the dock and is scrambling out of the boat before Charlie has a chance to tie it to the dock. "Hey, Charlie. Remember my daughter Meg? You met her a few weeks ago? And this is her friend Brian. They are *visiting*," he says with an emphasis on the last word.

We look at Charlie whose eyes appear as large as the mini pancakes at Rosie's. "Uh, yeah, right, Paul. I remember. Of course I remember. Good to see you again, Meg. Please enjoy your stay." He runs back to the kayak stand and pulls out his cellphone. Brian and I exchange looks.

"Dang it, Meg! Why'd you have to paddle so fast? Are you trying to kill me?" Dad coughs and coughs. I feel

141

bad but also irritated that this all could have been avoided if he'd just tell me the truth!

I can count on one hand how many times my dad has yelled at me: once for using Officer Toby's car for that joy ride, once for letting a feared bully copy my math test in sixth grade, and once for breaking up with Will, but he's apologized for that last one. I'm so surprised I don't have anything to say in return.

"Mr. Popkin—*Paul*—Meg was paddling like a maniac to mess with me. You remember my terrifying fear of the water?"

"I've heard something about it, yes," says Dad.

"She was trying to use the baptized by fire approach, trying to confront me with my fear smack in the face, if you will. So, it's my fault, really. I'm sorry."

Brian looks so dopey staring at my dad, his eyes downcast as if he's truly embarrassed for a completely ridiculous made-up story about the dangers of water on a perfectly calm, clear lake.

"Oh, well, I guess, I'm sorry," Dad stammers. "I overreacted a bit." His phone beeps. He pulls it out of his shorts pocket. Whatever he reads puts a giant smile on his face. "Everything is okay. Yes, everything is perfect," he says though we know he's regurgitating the text he's just read. "Let's enjoy this beautiful day." This time Dad puts his arm through Brian's and walks toward the nearest store, a thrift shop with an enthusiastic greeter outside the front door. And just like that, all is well with the world. But it's not. At all.

Chapter 17

Dad takes Brian to the electronics section of the thrift store. I check out the books, a mismatched assortment of bookshelves housing the collection with Danielle Steele shelved next to a raggedy covered Bible next to a How to Wallpaper Your Bathroom book. It's always a great buy to find books at a thrift shop. I pick out a book on knitting because you can never be too old to start a new hobby.

"Look what I found," says Brian proudly as he holds up a grotesque lamp with the base of the silhouette of a woman holding open a book. "Smart girl lamp!" he says grinning. "All I need is a new shade."

"That is the ugliest home décor I have ever seen."

"That's saying something coming from someone who decorated her kitchen sink with chicken nuggets."

"It was my trash can and *funny*. Where's Dad?"

"I'm not sure. He took me to the electronics section, but then he disappeared."

"You lost my dad?"

"I guess I did. Should we look for him?"

"I'm sure he's fine. He's a grown man."

"Excuse me?" A short elderly woman taps me on my arm. "Are you Meg?"

My heart begins to race. "Yes."

"Your father left this note for me to give you." She hands me a folded piece of paper.

"What's it say?" asks Brian as he looks over my shoulder.

Had to run out a minute. Meet me at the condo in an hour. Take the bikes back. Please go straight there. Thanks. 143 Dad

"What's *143* mean?" asks Brian.

I don't really want to tell him, both embarrassing and sentimental, but something about the true curiosity in his eyes tips the truth to his favor. "It means *I love you.* 1=I, 4=LOVE, 3=YOU—the number of letters. It's just something silly my family started using especially when Lara and I got too old for mushiness spoken out loud or around other people."

"I think it's sweet."

We lock eyes for a moment too long, and I forget the purpose of our trip. "I...I think we need to visit *Hope Street*," I say as I break away from Brian's gaze.

"Hope Street?"

I realize the ridiculousness of what I've said, but it's still true. There is something weird going on at the end of that street or the middle of the street at least, and I need to find out what it is. I fill him in on the mysterious street I'd been denied information about on my last visit as we walk toward the bicycles. I reach for one of the old red bicycles when an attendant who seems to appear out of nowhere brings me a blue one instead. "Here you go, Miss. I think you'll like this bicycle better. And there's an identical one for you, sir," he says to Brian. We know better than to argue again. We already know something crazy is going on with the colors. That part of the puzzle is clear.

As we near the giant speed bump in the road that signifies our arrival at Hope Street, I slow my pedaling. Streams of people head down the street, some not even bothering to use the sidewalk but instead walking down the middle of the road.

Ring. Ring. Rinnnnnggggg. Brian lays on his bell. "Shall we take a left?" he asks like a gleeful child.

I shake my head *no*. "I don't think we can. Look." I point in the direction of what I can only assume are the red color police.

"Oh, yeah, those dudes won't let us go down there."

Two men, large enough to be both bouncers at an exclusive club in Chicago and body doubles for The Rock stand on either side of the street. They try to blend in—one "reading" a book and the other "trimming" bushes that appear as if they aren't even real—but they aren't fooling us. They are security. I can't believe I missed them before.

"We'll have to come back tonight and figure something out."

"How do we get away without your dad finding out?"

"I don't know, but the key to this craziness is on Hope Street. I just know it."

The theme song to Jaws starts playing, and Brian takes out his phone. I can hear his end of the conversation.

Jerry?

Yeah, I'm good.

Really? Wow, thanks.

But I'm not sure I can get back in time.

Yeah, uh, I'm out of the state. Yeah, I understand it's a big deal, but…

I start motioning to Brian when I realize what Jerry is offering. *"It's okay,"* I mouth. *"We can go tonight."*

Brian shakes his head *no* at me. But I insist. Jerry is presenting a peace offering. He's asking him to fill in for the anchor tomorrow morning on the Sunday broadcast. Brian's time-out is over.

Dad is waiting at his condo after we hand in our bikes. He doesn't look upset at all or disappointed. It's almost like he is relieved that we are leaving. I admit it's not a cool feeling at all to know your dad wants you to go, but he never says anything like that, of course.

"I'll come back soon," I promise as I hug him goodbye, still thinner than I'm used to.

He clears his throat. "You are always welcome, Meg. But don't worry about it. I'm doing great. And, you, Brian, are welcome as well. Glad to see Meg has found such a good friend."

He winks at me. I ignore it. "You know, you can come back, too—to the city—and stay with Lara or me. We'd love to see you visit home again."

Dad doesn't say anything. He bobs his head in a half-hearted attempt at agreement.

"Take care of my little girl," Dad says to Brian as he clasps his hand.

Brian smiles while I roll my eyes. "I'll do that, Paul. You know she's a troublemaker and needs a shining knight to watch out for the princess."

"Okay, you two. Time to go," I say. "My carriage remote start began five minutes ago. Plus, *my acquaintance* has to get to work." I tug at Brian's sleeve and pull him toward the door.

"I'll be sure to stream the broadcast!" says Dad as we walk out into the hall. "Let me know when you're home safely!" Dad waves goodbye.

I let Brian drive the first half of the trip. I stare out the window as we pass fields being planted, the buds of fruit trees blooming, and the barrenness of the landscape that separates my dad from the rest of his family.

"I'm really sorry again for screwing up your weekend," Brian says as we pass a house with a political flag from the last presidential election cycle.

I look at him, the sun shining through the car window and highlighting his face with a true and gentle look of apology. "I know you are. But I couldn't deny Chicago the next nightly news star."

"Let's not go that far yet. It's a fill-in spot for a sick anchor on a Sunday morning after an imposed sabbatical."

"True, but you have to start somewhere. After you filled in for Steve a month ago, I heard the buzz. Numbers looked good. Jerry was impressed."

Brian stares forward, the playful look on his face dropping. "I don't know if I can do it again," he says at barely a whisper.

"What do you mean?" I sit up straighter and face him.

"After what happened…"

"You mean the shooting?"

Brian sighs deeply. "Yeah. News in a big city sucks a lot of the time. And this time it hit too close to home."

"Well, that's why you have reporters like me who try to shine a light on the positive things that happen in the city, too. Chicago has a lot of great stories."

Brian shakes his head. "I guess we make a good team then, huh?"

I don't answer. I don't have to. He knows I think so, too.

"Potty break?" he asks, pointing to a rest stop.

I pull into the no parking zone in front of Brian's condo building just after 11:00. The city is lit up like a brilliant Christmas tree and alive with Saturday night activity. "Thanks again," I say. "And good luck tomorrow morning. You'll do great."

"Be careful on the way to Brookfield. Text me when you're back, okay?"

"Okay, *Dad*." I say, appreciative of his care even though I'm much too old to be worried about while I'm driving.

"I had fun with you today. I haven't laughed that much in a long time."

"I had a decent time, too."

Brian reaches out and touches my hair, wrapping his fingers through the strands. He leans closer, pauses to wait for me to move away, but I don't. His gentle lips touch mine, and he kisses me tenderly but firmly. I close my eyes, and for a brief moment all worries in life slip away.

When we separate, I can feel my heart beating. I think I can hear Brian's too.

"We'll go back," he whispers. "I'm going back to Hope Street with you. I promise. "

I shake my head in agreement.

"And the flowers? Those were from me."

Then he's gone, pulling his duffle bag from the back seat. I watch him walk into the building and wonder if what I've just done will have unintended consequences. Then I catch a look of myself in the rearview mirror and see that I am smiling.

Chapter 18

"Hey, Meg," says Jerry as he walks by my cubicle. "Nice reporting on the break-ins on Michigan Ave. Your interview with the customer that was in the Old Navy when the robbery occurred was particularly good. You captured her raw feelings. Those kids need to be stopped. They are causing havoc around the city."

"Thanks, Jerry. It was a pretty traumatizing experience for her."

"I imagine so. I also was wondering if you've given any more thought as to what you want to do next," he says after he takes a swig from his coffee mug.

"Next?"

"Yes. The hospice story brought up our Thursday night ratings. The station would like to see what other feature story ideas you might have."

"Wow, that's great."

"So, I need a list of ideas by Monday."

"Monday?" The word catches in my throat as I've been so distracted with Dad and his move to Blue Lake, not to mention navigating around Brian at work without being awkward or raising any suspicions with my co-workers that something has happened between us. I haven't given much thought to new features. I'm disappointed in myself. These are the stories that excite me and give me passion for my work. These are the stories that show the beauty of Chicagoland. I should have a list ready to hand Jerry right now.

"Is that a problem?" Jerry asks, raising an eyebrow. "I thought you loved these kinds of stories."

"No, of course not. Not a problem at all. In fact, I have so many ideas I just need to pare them down," I smile too widely.

"Great. I look forward to seeing the list on Monday." He walks back to his office.

"On Monday," I repeat after he's already gone.

"You don't have a list, do you?" Jessalyn stands next to me smirking, her too tight dress holding up her breasts in an unnaturally high position.

"I have lots of ideas, Jessa. I don't just read a teleprompter. I *write* my stories."

She glares at me before stomping away down the hall. Man, I hate that woman.

When she is out of eyesight, I slump my upper body onto my desk. Why didn't I keep my mouth shut? *Too many ideas?* What is wrong with me?

It's a slow day in Chicago which is nearly unheard of, so the gods must be smiling down on me as I spend the entire afternoon Googling ideas and looking through old story contacts trying to find an interesting story. My list so far is slim including:

A librarian on the north side who's been working for forty years and the progression of book banning she's observed during the course of her career

A student at Lane Tech College Prep who created a homework tutor app with high school students helping other students

A neighborhood watch group which has grown to include beautification of the neighborhood that had unintended consequences of actually lowering crime because of the investment in the area

A group of former star high school athletes who visit schools in an effort to educate about the dangers of drug use

It's not that I find the story ideas unworthy because they are all well-meaning. The problem is *my* passion. It's lacking at the moment, but Jerry needs a list of ideas, and I have to give him the list if I want to keep my job—at least long enough to find another story idea like the hospice story that *does* give me passion.

Meet me on the roof in ten

I read my text message and close my eyes. *Brian.* It's not like we've purposely tried to avoid each other since the weekend, but ever since Brian's hiatus ended, he's been thrown back into work. And even though my assignments have been relatively mundane—car accidents, thefts, a new penguin born at the aquarium—our paths haven't crossed often. I suppose now is as good a time as any to discuss what happened—what happened *again* as we never talked about the first time that Brian kissed me in my apartment after Linda almost killed him. Plus, I have writer's block and need some fresh air. I shut down my laptop, notice the time—11:45—and realize an early lunch is not out of the question.

I take the elevator to the rooftop. Ten or fifteen people from the building are sitting at tables or lounging on outdoor couches eating lunch. Brian raises his hand and waves me over. He looks so handsome with the sun illuminating through his hair. The tie around his neck is loosened and the top button on his gray button down shirt is undone. Maybe if we didn't work together this might be a spark worth pursuing. The spark is hard to deny. But nothing can happen between us. We *work* together.

"Hey, Meg. You look great!" says Brian as he stands up from his chair to greet me with a hug.

Why does he have to smell good, too, a mixture of woodsy and leather? "Thanks, Brian," I say as I flatten my flowy skirt before I sit down. "It's really nice up here."

"Nicer now that you're here."

"Thanks, but…we…can…"

Brian puts a finger to my lips. "Don't say anything yet. Just enjoy the fresh air and the view, and for once I'm not meaning staring at me."

I laugh because it's easy to laugh with Brian. There's still a hint of arrogance under the surface, but now that I've seen his vulnerability, I know it's a charade. Plus, his self-deprecation is cute. I wait for him to speak.

"I wanted to apologize again for having to leave Blue Lake so quickly. I know you wanted to see what was happening at Hope Street and also visit more with your dad. There's definitely something odd happening in that town."

"It's okay. You had to take the opportunity to get back to work. Honestly, I think Dad was ready to have me out of his hair. I was snooping and he sensed it."

Brian nods in agreement. "Yeah, you're probably right." He clears his throat at the same time that a cloud covers the sun, and his illuminance is gone. "But I won't apologize for kissing you."

I sit up straighter and put a hand on his arm. "Brian, we can't…"

"Stop it. Yes, we *can*. We *can,* Meg. I just can't be your subordinate, and you can't be mine. I looked at the station's handbook."

"It's too risky," I argue. "You weren't here when a bunch of people were fired for inappropriate staff relationships. Plus, you're on thin ice with Jerry, Brian. He told you that if you embarrass the station again, you're gone. The last thing he wants is some awkward story about his reporters dating."

Brian grabs my hand, but I pull it away before anyone notices. "You're worth the risk."

It's been so long since anyone has made me feel the way that Brian Welter makes me feel. "I don't know what else to say," I whisper.

"That's fine. You don't have to say anything right now. But let me make up for last weekend. A buddy of mine has season tickets with his wife to Wrigley Field, and he can't go to the game tomorrow afternoon. Come with me." He pauses. "The seats are behind the first base line." He smiles, his dimples dancing on his face.

"I do *love* the Chicago Cubs. But we can't call it a date. Okay?"

"You can call it a funeral if you want to. I don't care as long as I'm there with you."

"Deal. Text me the details, and I'll meet you at the visitation." I wink. As I walk away, I know he's watching me, and I like it.

Chapter 19

I nearly miss the train from Brookfield into the city, rushing around my apartment trying to find my Cubs t-shirt. I find it hanging in the back of my closet, placed there after the last baseball game I attended with Will. The game had been delayed for an hour because of rain. Will got so impatient that he drank three beers super quickly, got drunk, and dumped his nachos in my lap. I spent so much time in the bathroom trying to wash off the sticky cheese that I missed the first three outs of the Cardinals and the first two Cubs batters hitting home runs.

I glance at myself in the reflection of the train windows. I've pulled my hair back on the sides with a Cubs barrette I found buried in my bedside table. I'd left a few strands hanging around my face and made sure to add lip gloss with sun protection. I don't know why I tried so hard to look *cute* or whatever look I'm going for. Brian is my friend. *My friend.*

When I get off the train, Brian is waiting for me with a Starbucks drink. "Hey, sunshine. Thirsty?" He waves the Starbucks in front of him.

"Depends. What are you offering?"

He laughs evilly. "Do you want the real answer to that question?"

"Give me the damn drink," I say, shaking my head. "How much time do we have?"

"We're good on time. The 'L' stop is a few blocks north."

"Then we take the Red Line into Wrigleyville."

"Right, my city girl. Why are you asking *me?* You're the local." He raises his hands in the air.

"True. Let's go then. Maybe if we get there early enough, we'll get the promotion prize. I looked online. Today they're giving out Ron Santo replica statues to the first 10000 spectators."

"Ron *who?*"

"Come on. I'll explain on the train." I grab Brian's hand and pull him through the crowds on the sidewalk. It seems natural, leading my friend to our next stop.

The train is packed with baseball fans. There are no seats left when we get onboard at Grand Avenue. I grab hold of a center pole to balance myself. Brian stands behind me. His body falls onto mine every time the train jerks. I can feel his warm breath on my neck and wonder what it would be like to pretend we weren't *just friends*.

We snag our Ron Santo statues as we enter the gates of Wrigley Field, Brian pledging his to my dad who will be most grateful. He was the first person, after all, who introduced me to his beloved Cubbies. Wrigley Field will always hold a special place in my heart. The ivy is in full bloom this June afternoon along the outfield fence with the sun beating with intensity on the bleachers. Brian's tickets are behind first base but under the top deck, so we are protected from the sun.

"I don't know if they have wine, but I'm going to grab a beer. Want anything?" he asks as we await the start of the game.

"I *prefer* wine, but you can't come to Wrigley without drinking a beer. Thanks."

While I'm waiting, I get a text from Lara.

Dad isn't answering my calls.

Weird.

Have you heard from him?

Not for a couple of days.

Nolan's birthday party is tomorrow.

Right.

Did you forget, too?

I can hear her swearing from her expensive house on the north side, letting loose about how forgetful or self-centered or whatever adjective she chooses to fling at us. I have barely recovered from the abuse I received when I forgot to call Blake on his fourth birthday *three years* ago.

Didn't forget at all. At the Cubs game now.

Whoa. By yourself?

With a friend.

Huh. Oh, wait! Dad just texted. Thank God. See you tomorrow. Don't be late.

"Why the sour face?" Brian asks as he hands me a beer, 22 ounces, and way more beer than I've ever had in a single serving.

"Wow! That's big!"

"You're *welcome!*"

"Thanks. My sister texted. She hadn't heard from Dad but then she did and all is well."

"Sounds dramatic." His eyes twinkle with merriment and I'm lost for a moment.

"She isn't called the drama queen in the family for no reason, but she did have a valid concern. Dad's phone is nearly attached to his hand. It's odd that neither of us heard from him for a couple of days."

"Do you think you should go see him again?"

"I'll see him tomorrow, so it's probably nothing to worry about."

"Oh, I didn't know you were going to Michigan tomorrow."

"I'm not. Dad's coming to Illinois. My nephew's second birthday party is tomorrow afternoon."

"Oh, cool. I'll give him the Ron Santino statue then," he says, holding up the collector's box he'd taken out from under his seat.

"Ron *Santo*," I say. "And you are *not* going to my nephew's birthday party."

Brian takes a long swig of his equally large beer before answering. "I'll text your dad. He'll put me on the invite list." He pulls out his phone.

"Stop it!" I yell, grabbing hold of his arm. He spills some of his beer which splashes onto my face and down my neck.

"That's what you get!" His eyes display his evil playfulness. "Let me help you clean that up." And he reaches over and covers my cheek with kisses that make my heart flutter. But when he kisses my neck my heart just stops. I am paralyzed.

We miss the first two batters because we can't stop staring at each other. Neither of talks until the second inning because it will only lead to more protestations from me that this will never work. But when the balls start flying off the bats, we find our groove. We high-five the people around us when the Cubs score four runs in the sixth inning and lace arms around each other's backs to sing the seventh inning stretch, *Take Me Out to the Ball Game*. Brian buys me pink cotton candy, and I finish my beer. He orders another. He even shags a foul ball and gives it to a little girl sitting in front of us.

"Jealous?"

"Nope," I'd said. "That's about the sweetest thing I've ever seen."

After the game we go to a bar in Wrigleyville. I order a pinot, and Brian orders a rum and Coke. We try to play pool with another couple, but I'm so tipsy I keep missing the ball. Brian stands behind me holding the stick steady long enough for me to strike the ball. We lose, but I don't care. It doesn't matter. I'm having one of the best days I've had in years, and I don't want it to end. We eat fried chicken strips at the bar and switch to water. Brian tells me more about his life, his professor dad and his Army mom, about how he'd learned to act tough so he wouldn't be swallowed up every time he was the new kid in school because the family moved around so much. And it took his younger sister getting pregnant at eighteen before he'd softened up a little. "That kid is the lifeblood of our family."

I learn about his early years playing football when he'd been pummeled by a ten-year-old boy when he was only eight that had terrified him so badly he'd switched to baseball and found success as a catcher until his knee blew out in his freshman year of college and he'd needed surgery. He asks me questions, too, and what impresses me the most is that he really listens—maybe because he's a trained journalist—but it feels like he really cares to learn that I'd peed my pants while on stage at my first dance recital and caused a puddle that lead to a train wreck of little girls in tutus slipping and falling to the floor. My sides are hurting from laughing so much by the time we exit the train where we'd actually gotten seats this time because most of the baseball spectators had scattered to their homes.

"Thanks for a great day, Brian. I have to catch the Metra line to Brookfield, so I'd better get going. I have twenty minutes to make it. Thanks again." I feel my face getting warm, much warmer than the rest of me that is chilled. I turn in the direction of my next train so he doesn't notice, but he pulls me around by wrapping his arm around my waist and drawing me toward his body.

"Don't go, Meg," he whispers against my hair. "Stay with me tonight. Please. I make a killer night cap."

"The last thing I need is more alcohol. I'm finally seeing straight again." I tell myself I should go, but it feels so good to be held right now that I don't have the desire to fight with doing the right thing.

Brian starts moving me in the direction of his condo.

"I can't, Brian. I…shouldn't."

"I'm not going to force you to do anything you don't want to do," says Brian, releasing his hold on me with everything but his eyes.

And that's all I need to hear to change my mind. He reaches out his hand, and I take it. We walk quickly now, perhaps because of the cold, but more likely because of the anticipation of being alone.

Brian's condo is small but clean. Everything seems to have a place and a purpose. The plants face the windows. The dishes are stacked neatly on an open shelf. I suppose you learn order when you have a military mom. Brian points out the bathroom. A desert scene is pictured on his shower curtain, and his soap dispenser is a cactus. I smile.

He's changed into a pair of sweatpants and a tight white t-shirt when I come out of the bathroom after splashing water on my face and finger brushing my teeth from a half-used tube I'd found in a drawer. He hands me a glass of water—extra ice—when I join him on the balcony that overlooks the city. Dad has a beautiful view in Blue Lake, but Brian has a breathtaking view with lights in every direction, traffic sounds and music from a club below, and if you crane your neck just so he has a peek of Lake Michigan where the lights from yachts bounce in the harbor. "It's gorgeous," I say, leaning on the railing.

"No, you're gorgeous, Meg."

He holds me tightly with his arms wrapped around me from behind, both of us mesmerized by the view and feel of each other's body so close. I turn to face him. He touches my face so tenderly I think I might crumble to the floor of the balcony. He pulls my lips to his. He kisses me softly, but as we push our bodies toward each other I feel his excitement through his sweatpants, and I kiss him more fervently. We stumble back into the condo and into his bedroom, tripping over a laundry basket full of his perfectly folded clothes.

"Do you have protection?" I ask breathlessly.

"I do." His breath matches mine. He reaches over me to his nightstand and pulls out a box of condoms. He raises my arms above my head and removes my Cubs t-shirt. I wriggle out of my shorts. He takes off his sweatpants and t-shirt. I run my hands over his chest. He kisses my neck reaching around my back to unlatch my bra. "You're breathtaking," he says as his kisses fall to my breasts. He enters so gently as I fall backwards to the pillow that catches my head. And soon we are one. He lets me climax first, a release I didn't know I needed—and wanted—so badly. And when he comes moments later, we collapse together on the bed. He holds me close, and I let him.

Chapter 20

"Shit!" I sit up in bed as the sun bores down from a set of floor-to-ceiling windows. It takes me a half second to remember where I am.

Brian rolls over, "Well, good morning to you, too."

"I'm sorry! I am! I'm supposed to be at Nolan's birthday party by noon." I look at the clock in a panic. "That's an hour away. I don't have time to go home. She'll kill me. She'll kill me. Lara will *kill* me!"

"Meg, calm down." Brian rubs my back. "We'll get you there. Go take a shower."

I jump out of bed and run to the bathroom. I don't even have time to process what happened last night. I find a towel under the sink and let the water wash over me. It's the worst shower of my life as I realize I have two new problems. One, I have nothing to wear. Two, Nolan's gift—a miniature train set—is sitting on my kitchen table in Brookfield. I shut off the shower and wrap myself up in a towel. I walk back to the bedroom and spy my wrinkled Cubs shirt and shorts sitting in a pile on the floor. Brian is typing on his laptop. He tosses me a St. Patrick's Day shirt. It's June. This is not helping. He closes his computer.

"I know. Sorry. It's the only shirt I have that's too small for me. Everything else fits my muscles perfectly." He flexes.

"That is not helpful."

His eyes crinkle with pride. "Sorry. You just need to wear it for as long as it takes to get you something more appropriate. Though the idea of you standing by my side all day and *not* wearing panties is kind of exciting. Do you think there's any wiggle room in this schedule today?"

I toss a pillow at his head, but he catches it. "Put on your bra and shorts. And don't forget the sexy t-shirt I gave you. We've got a quick trip to Target to make."

"Are you serious?"

"As serious as Jerry on a deadline," he says. "I Google mapped Target and back. We can make the round-trip trip in eighteen minutes if we hurry. Let's go!"

I towel dry my hair, throw on the clothes I have at the minute and follow Brian to the elevator. He stares at me with a dopey grin as we wait for the elevator to arrive. "Do I have a giant booger or something?"

"Nope, at least not on the outside of your nose."

"Then why are you staring?"

"I just can't believe I got to wake up next to such a beautiful woman today."

"I imagine that's the same line you give all the other girls that wake up here." It comes out of my mouth before I can stop it.

Brian looks hurt. He doesn't speak to me as the elevator doors open. "Brian, I'm sorry. I didn't mean it. I'm just really stressed right now."

"I don't sleep around, Meg. Despite what you may think I haven't slept with *anyone* since I've been in Chicago."

"I know. I mean—I *didn't* know. I thought Jessalyn—at least I'd heard…"

"I haven't slept with *anyone* since I've been in Chicago, no matter what you've heard."

"I'm sorry. Forgive me."

"On one condition," he says, his smile returning.

"Anything. Uh…maybe. What's the condition?"

"You have to take me to the birthday party."

"You've got to be kidding. Dad barely bought the *we're just friends* thing when in Blue Lake. He definitely won't believe me if you show up to his grandson's birthday party."

"But we *were* just friends. Now we're l…o…v…e…r…s!"

"Damn. I am in real trouble today."

At Target I grab two summer dresses, one a solid yellow sleeveless dress that falls just above my knees and the other a white sleeveless dress with an eyelet design. I buy cheap sandals, and despite Brian's desire, I buy a package of bikini underwear. I pick up foundation, moisturizer, mascara, lip gloss, and a toothbrush. "This is the most expensive birthday party I've ever been to."

"And you've forgotten the most important part of a birthday party."

"The present," we both say at the same time.

"You get in line, and I'll pick something out," Brian says.

"But you don't know what to get."

He wrinkles his forehead when he looks at me. "I'm the only one here who's been a little boy. Plus, my niece is nine, so I've had plenty of experience in the cool uncle role."

I don't argue because the clock is ticking down.

"Excuse me, so sorry. I'm with that pretty girl over there!" I hear from behind as Brian joins me in line. Why is it so busy today?

"Aren't you Brian Welter from WDOU?" *Oh no.*

"Oh, yeah, hello, yes. Sorry to butt in front of you. I'm with this…"

"Pretty girl?" the woman repeats Brian's sentence.

I turn around. The woman's face brightens. "Oh my gosh! You're Meg Popkin. You guys are so cute. I didn't know you were a couple! Let me get a pic!" She pulls out her phone and snaps a picture before either of us can stop her.

"It's okay!" Brian yells as we race back to his condo. "Meg, stop running! I'll talk to Jerry Monday morning. There's no way he's going to see the picture. If we get ahead of this and tell him we're dating, he can't be upset. He just doesn't like surprises. Meg, stop!"

He pulls the back of my—*his*—shirt. I stop running, but I can't stop the tears that are sliding down my face. Brian tugs me into his building before anyone else can snap a picture. When we are safely in the elevator again, he pulls me into his chest and lets me cry. I haven't cried since my mom's funeral, and I don't know why I'm crying now. I love my job. I don't want to lose my job because we didn't disclose our relationship. I didn't even know we had a relationship. Do I have a relationship? What is this? What am I doing? The thoughts tumble in my head like the long cycle on a washing machine.

I take a deep breath and nod. "I'm sorry. I just don't want there to be any repercussions that get either of us in trouble at work."

"Everything is going to be okay. But we have to go now unless you want repercussions from your big sister."

"Thanks," I whisper. "I don't even know what you bought Nolan."

"It's all under control. Trust me. I've got some wrapping paper. You get ready. I'll wrap the present. Then I'll drive. It will be faster than the train. Traffic is light on Sundays, too."

"Okay, thanks. And, um, sorry about that." I point to the snot stain on Brian's t-shirt.

"Huh. Good thing I did laundry yesterday. Go!" He points to the bathroom.

I choose the white eyelet dress, apply my makeup quickly, and brush my teeth. My hair has dried and has a mind of its own, so I rummage through my purse for a hair tie. I brush it back and pull it into a messy knot. It will have to do. "Brian, do you have a plastic bag I can carry my stuff in when you drop me off later?"

"Sure, but leave that here."

I look at my hand. Brian is pointing to my toothbrush. "Brian, I don't know if we're…"

"Leave it here. Let's go."

Brian drives a little faster than you should on a Sunday morning in Chicago, but we arrive safely and almost on schedule.

"Well, look who the cat dragged in!" says Lara as Brian and I arrive *fifteen* minutes late.

"Sorry, I'm late." A kiss on the cheek shuts her up for a minute.

I ignore her raised eyebrow at Brian.

"Hello, Brian. I didn't know we'd be seeing you today," says Dad as he shakes Brian's hand.

"Nor did I," whispers Lara in my ear.

"Lara, Rick, this is my friend Brian."

"Brian, this is my sister Lara and brother-in-law Rick."

After the adult greetings and exchange of the Ron Santo replica statue that makes my dad giddy like his grandsons, Rick takes them to the backyard to play with the boys. They seem to have an assortment of balls scattered around the lawn.

"Is that Brian Welter?" squeals my sister. "He's hot! You didn't tell me that Brian was your boyfriend!"

"You sound like a teenager. Seriously, Lara! And he's not my boyfriend. We're friends."

"Well, from the look of that hairdo, I'd say you're a little more than friends."

"I'm going to the backyard." I start to walk away, but Lara stops me.

"Wait. I'm sorry. I don't know how much time we'll have to talk alone, and I want to talk about Dad."

"Did you ask him why it took him so long to answer you yesterday?"

"I did, and he told me this crazy story about washing his phone and not having access to it, but that's a load of crap because he obviously answered me later in the day on the *same phone*, and we all know that phones don't dry out that fast or at all. And he's wobbly. He keeps holding on to things as he walks. He's been holding his head. I think he might be sick."

"That's not good." I sit down in the nearest chair.

"He seemed a bit unsteady in Blue Lake, now that you mention it, holding on to the wall before he stepped out to the balcony, but that's all I noticed. He seemed fine on the sidewalks and in the kayak, well, except for the coughing attack, but that's because he was trying to chase Brian and me in the kayak.

"Excuse me?" asks Lara.

"It sounds way worse than it actually was," I giggle.

"Just watch him. I think I'm going to ask him if he's sick. I wonder if that awful town has any decent doctors. If he's sick, he needs to be back here in Chicago where he can get the best care."

I look outside. Dad is laughing at something Rick is saying while Brian kicks a soccer ball back and forth with the boys. I sure wish Mom was here to see all of us together like this. She'd have been so proud.

After a lunch of hotdogs and hamburgers, Nolan opens his gifts. Dad gives him a new set of giant Legos that his brothers eagerly rip open. "Ooh, what did Auntie Meg get you, Nolan?" asks Dad.

"Train," he says.

Ahh…he knows me so well, but that train will now have to be his Christmas gift. Nolan rips the paper in small pieces until the toy that Brian purchased is revealed. I throw my hands over my face in horror.

"Oh, man! That is the *best* gift ever!" says Rick who bursts into laughter. So does everyone else except for Lara and me—and Nolan, who has no idea what it is.

I whisper *I'm sorry* to Lara as Rick opens the box for his son. "Here, Nolan. Push this button."

Nolan dutifully obeys his dad, and a stuffed dog starts walking around the floor stopping to lift its leg and fart. And the purest giggle in the world fills the room.

Chapter 21

Brian and I compare notes about our texts before we arrive at work, each from our own homes.

See me.

That's it. The same message from Jerry arrived at 8:30 a.m. to both of us. My heart sinks as I open all of my social media accounts. Twitter. *Clear.* Facebook. *Clear.* Tik Tok. *Clear.* Instagram. *#WDOU.* And there it is. *Meg Popkin is dating new local talent, Brian Welter,* with a picture of us at Target, St. Patrick's Day shirt and all. Nothing says *walk of shame* more than wearing an oversized St. Patrick's Day shirt in June on a Sunday morning. My heart sinks.

Don't worry.

How could I not worry? We're going to be fired.

We are not getting fired, Meg.

You weren't here during #metoo when a bunch of people lost their jobs for having sex with co-workers.

Likely because they were subordinates, though, right?

Yeah, but we were drilled about doing everything in the open. No secrets.

We weren't trying to keep secrets. My charm swept you off your feet. :-)

Not LOL

I follow Brian down the hall to Jerry's office at the same time—8:30 a.m. sharp. Tom had given me a big hug when he saw me in the staff room earlier this morning. I guess news travels fast. Jessa stands outside Jerry's door smirking at both of us. We ignore her.

"Sit!" He points to the two chairs in front of his desk.

"Look, Jerry, we can explain," says Brian.

"It's not what it looks like!" I blurt out. "Brian and Rick, my brother-in-law, are friends. They're on the same baseball team." I don't even look at Brian while I'm talking. "We were shopping for my nephew's birthday party which was yesterday afternoon. It was a pool party, Jerry. I was wearing my swimsuit under that t-shirt. That's why I looked ridiculous. It is *not* what it looks like on the internet. I promise. Brian and I just went to the party together because I picked him up on my way. That's all. We are most certainly *not* dating." I'm nearly out of breath when I stop talking.

Jerry doesn't say anything. He looks at me for a long time. I don't blink. Then he looks at Brian. I wish I could do the same, but I can't. I know I've hurt him.

"Is that true, Brian?"

Brian clears his throat. "Well, Jerry, you heard Meg. You know her. She's not a liar, is she?"

It stings to hear Brian say that because that's exactly what he thinks of me. That's exactly what I am. Now I've moved away from one potentially bad situation and created a new one.

"Alright then. We'll ignore the story, some overzealous fan who got a shot of our reporters shopping for a little kid's birthday party. I can live with that. But you know I expect honesty. I took over this job because the last guy let things go on in this office that reeked of impropriety. Do you understand?"

"Yes, Jerry," I say. "Of course."

"And don't be seen together in public. It will lead to speculation."

Brian doesn't say anything. He leaves the office first without looking at me.

Tom and I cover a story at a casino outside the city that was robbed this morning. I don't care about the story, but I'm grateful for the distraction.

"Can you tell me what you were doing when the men in masks came into the room?" I ask a server who'd been working when three masked men barged into the casino carrying guns. Her black mascara has run down her face, evidence of the trauma she's been through today.

"I dropped to the floor like they told me to do. We've been trained not to resist. It's too risky. Plus, I knew a pit boss would have time to hit the panic button. One of the guys, the heavier one, pointed a gun at my head while the other demanded money from behind the counter. Police got here fast but not before they snatched a bunch of money."

"Do you have actual training for robberies like this, you mean?"

"Yeah, we talk about what would happen if…"

"Look, we don't need our security measures broadcast all over Chicagoland," a woman in a blue suit and heels says sternly as she waves her hand at the woman to return to work. "Get back to work, Bonnie. But clean up that face first!"

"Thank you for answering my questions," I say. The young woman smiles shyly as she hurries away. I turn my attention to the woman who I assume is management.

"Kind of callous of you to make your employee continue to work on the same day she's had a gun pointed at her head."

The woman's eyes get big before she squints them again and leans in close, "How dare you tell me how to run my business!"

Tom puts his hand on my arm. "Let's go, Meg. Sorry about this, Miss. I sure hope they catch those guys."

"Thanks," she says, her spit flying in Tom's face before he pulls me toward the exit.

"Bitch," I say under my breath.

Tom lets me have it in the van. "What the heck was that all about?" he asks. "Are you trying to get station complaints and get called into Jerry's office again?"

"No. Of course not! I didn't think. I'm angry. I'm sorry. You're right. Ugh. I've screwed everything up! But did you see that poor server?"

"Well, it's not *that* bad. That boss *is* a bitch." Tom winks before he starts the van.

I smile for the first time today.

"Thanks, friend."

"If I'm being a real friend, then I need you to know that you've really hurt your other *friend*."

"What do you mean?"

"Don't play dumb. I'm a cameraman. I'm paid to notice things. Brian is crazy about you. I don't know what happened with that internet picture or what happened in Jerry's office, but you need to make it right."

Chapter 22

I text Brian to meet me in the edit room, but when he hasn't shown up after fifteen minutes, I leave. I try to follow up on my list that might lead to another feature story idea, but I don't have the heart. And Jerry hasn't chastised me for being late with my list—yet. My thoughts return to the weekend and to the way Brian touched me when we made love, so gentle yet so knowing. And the way he'd gotten along with my family warmed my heart. Why didn't I tell Jerry the truth?

It's been a week since Brian last spoke with me. Jerry assigned stories that would not have us crossing paths, and no one in the office looked at us weird anymore except for Tom. It's not like I haven't tried. I've asked Brian to meet me on the roof countless times. I've called him at home. I even thought about taking the train into the city and just showing up at his place, but the thought of being rebuffed and not even being allowed into the building had stopped me. I miss him. I miss his goofy grins and confidence, knowing that just behind lies a caring soul who'd protect me and take care of me. I miss his smell as he pulls me close. How could I have been so stupid to have risked this relationship because I was afraid of Jerry and losing my job, of being relegated back to traffic stories when I'd worked so hard to be allowed to pursue my own interests or judged by my peers as only being interested in my hormones and not the real news stories I cared about? Why do I care so much what *other* people think instead of what makes *Meg* happy? And why didn't I give Brian a chance to explain to Jerry?

I think about trying to talk to him again when I see Brian walk past my desk after the 10:00 news ends. He'd done a live story from the studio about a new program at city hall that helps speed up the process of applying for unemployment. I actually get up and follow him from a distance, but Brian leaves the building and walks in the direction of Henry's. I want to follow him all the way there, confront him when he's stuck in the back of the bar with a beer in hand, goofing off with his friends, but I don't. I'm too proud to be publicly shamed when he snubs me. Plus, only a few steps behind him walks Jessalyn Bowers, leather pants and tube top flaunting her figure. Is she with Brian? Or following him? My heart hurts, but I'm a coward.

So, instead, I return to my cubicle for my backpack. In the bathroom I change into running pants, a tank top, and a light jacket and walk to the train station. A couple holding hands passes by. The woman is laughing at whatever the man is saying, and the man stares at her as if she's the only person on the sidewalk, so much so that I have to move out of the way so that they don't crash into me.

It's after 11:00 p.m. when I arrive at the train platform. The moon is quiet tonight, covered in hazy clouds, and there's a light out overhead. There aren't usually a lot of people on the platform at this time of night, but sometimes Jerry's administrative assistant rides the train part of the way with me. She's on maternity leave though—fourth baby. I shudder to imagine what that must be like.

It's late. All I want to do is get home to Linda and go to bed. I want to forget about the mess I've made at work and the mess I've made out of my relationship with Brian. My body is tired, and my senses are dulled, or I'd have realized I wasn't alone sooner. It's too late to go back to the station. The crude cat calls are close—too close. I don't dare turn around. I check my watch, ten more minutes before the train arrives. I reach into my pocket to pull out my pepper spray as I notice a shadow approaching on my right side. When I move closer to the train tracks, a large stick—*a golf club?*—comes crashing over the back of my head, and I go sprawling to the concrete floor of the train platform. It hurts. It hurts so bad. *Take her phone. Grab her bag.* Rifling through my bag. Giddiness. *Got it! A wallet. Let's go.*

I don't know how long I lie there. My body hurts. My head aches. I slowly reach to my head. My hand feels something wet, and I feel sick. I turn my head and vomit to the side. Then I close my eyes.

When I wake up, I am in bed, but it's not my own. Someone is shining a bright light into my eyes, and it makes my head hurt more. "Where am…?" My mouth is so dry it's hard to speak.

"Hello, Ms. Popkin. You are at Cook County Hospital. Can you answer a few questions for me?"

I shake my head *yes*. "Can you tell me what year it is?"

"2023."

"Good. And where do you work?"

"News…WDOU, Chicago's most trustworthy source for news," I say, adding the station's tagline.

The man I presume to be the doctor laughs. "I think that's a great answer. Good thing, too, since you're likely to become a story *on* the news tomorrow instead of telling it."

"Oh, no. What happened…?"

But he doesn't answer as the door opens behind him. "Oh, Meg! How is she? Is she okay?" Jerry rushes to the side of my bed. He grabs my hand and looks earnestly at the doctor.

"She's got a nasty gash on her head from where she was struck and received some stitches for that. Otherwise, she has bruising from her collision with the platform. She's lucky. The last time these brutes sent someone to my hospital the patient ended up in rehab for six months because of brain damage."

"No." It's not Jerry who is talking. I try to turn my head to the voice, but it hurts too much.

"She's going to be okay?" Jerry asks the doctor.

"She's going to be fine physically though pretty sore for a few days. We have a victim's representative who will talk to her when she's stronger to give her some resources for therapy. I'd highly recommend she talk to someone. What she's been through is very traumatic."

"Thanks, Doctor."

I raise my hand like I'm in elementary school, so everyone realizes that I—the source of these discussions—am still here and conscious. "Can I have some water?"

The doctor smiles with gentle eyes. "Absolutely. I'll send someone in with that. I'll be back in the morning to check on you before my shift ends. You'll have lots of staff popping in to bug you for your vitals. Take care, Ms. Popkin."

"Thank you."

"Okay, Brian. I'm going to talk to the administration about keeping our competitors off of this floor. Meg doesn't need anyone bothering her. Plus, this story is *ours*. Can you stay with her until her sister arrives?"

"Jerry, that's kind of harsh."

Brian.

"We don't have to make this a story. We can cover it as an anonymous victim."

Brian.

"We *could*, but that's not how the news works all the time," Jerry says.

"You mean, that's not the way *ratings* work, Jerry. That's a bitch of a thing to do to your employee."

Brian.

"Sorry, Brian. That's reality. I'll text you later." I hear the door close.

Brian. He's here.

"Oh, Meg," he says, bending down so that his face is in front of mine. "Why are you crying?"

I reach my hand to my face and feel the tears as they fall. I'm so tired.

When I wake up again, Lara is sitting at my bedside. "Meg! Oh, my *Meg*. How are you, honey?" She touches my cheek softly. "I was so worried about you."

"What happened?"

She turns around to look at someone behind her.

"Hi, Meg."

Brian.

Brian takes my hand. "You don't remember anything?" he asks gently.

I shake my head which is throbbing. "I left...I left work. I was going to the train. The light was out on the platform. *That's it.* That's all I remember."

"Okay. You don't need all the details. You were hit over the head, and someone stole your phone and wallet, but you're going to be fine. I promise."

When I look up from his hand that feels so gentle, tears are pooling in his eyes. "My phone?"

Lara sighs, exasperated. "I told you the first thing she'd worry about was her phone!"

"We'll get you a new phone. It's password protected. They just want to wipe it and sell it again anyway. No one will see your naked pictures." He laughs, his teary eyes twinkling.

"Meg, I'm going back home for a short bit. Rick has to go to work, and I'll take the boys to a friend's house. Then I'll come right back. I promise. Okay? Brian said he'd stay with you. You're a lucky woman," she says patting Brian on the arm.

"Okay. Can I have some water?"

"I've got it, Lara. Thanks."

"And you'll let me know if there's a change—*anything?*"

"Of course I will. I promise. Say hello to Rick for me."

"Okay, I will. Thanks again. Meg is lucky to have you."

When Lara is gone Brian takes a chair and pulls it closer to my bed. He sits down and holds my hand again.

"I didn't think you were talking to me," I say slowly, smiling.

"I wish I was still not talking to you because then you'd be safe and not lying in a hospital with a gash in your head."

"I had to get your attention somehow." My voice sounds so weak.

"Well, it worked."

"Brian, I'm sorry. I never should have lied to Jerry. I got scared one of us would lose our job or be demoted or something. I completely overreacted, recalling a time at the station when people *did* lose their jobs because of their relationships, but I know that was different. There were bosses involved with subordinates, married staff having affairs. This is totally different. I'm so sorry."

"I understand your reasons. I really do. I did then, too, actually. It's just that you didn't tell me you were going to say those things to Jerry, and it felt like you were denying *us*, that you and I being together wasn't real."

I squeeze Brian's hand. "It was real."

"Good."

"Why did you come with Jerry?"

"He texted me at Henry's."

"But why *you*?"

"Because I told him a week ago that I was in love with you."

"Brian, I…you…"

"Shh…get some rest. We can talk about this later. I'm going to get you some more ice."

And then he is gone, leaving me to try to process what he's said, what I've been through, what happens next.

Chapter 23

"I'm fine, Dad. Really, I am. Yeah, it was scary, but I don't remember everything. I got a big konk on my head to thank for the memory loss. Yes, the police interviewed me in the hospital this morning. No, they haven't arrested anyone yet. No, don't come. Lara's here. Yes, Brian's been here, too. I think a trip to Blue Lake would be nice, too. Yes, we'll come soon. I promise. Love you, too, Dad." I push the red button on my phone.

"You're a popular girl," Lara says as she helps me wash my face in the bathroom sink of my hospital room. "First Tom and now Dad."

"Tom and Anita are so sweet. I had to thank them for the flowers. Aren't they beautiful?"

"They are very pretty. A lot of people care about you. Dad's really worried about you."

"I know he is. But we're worried about him, too," I say, handing Lara a brush for the rat's nest in my hair. "Be careful. Stay away from my stitches."

She takes the brush and begins to gently untangle my hair. Flashbacks of Mom brushing my hair as a little girl linger in my mind. I wish she were here now. I wish she could hug me and tell me everything would be okay, that life would get easier, that good always wins out in the end.

"He tries so hard to be cheerful," she says.

"Do you think that's true, or does that place have some sort of weird magical hold over him that *makes* him cheerful—no trying needed?"

"I don't know."

"Did Dad mention anything to you about Hope Street?"

"No. What's that?"

"Ouch!"

"Sorry! I'm so sorry. I'll be more careful. Your hair is a disaster, Sis."

"Thanks, Captain Obvious."

"What's Hope Street?"

"I'm not sure. I noticed it the first time I visited after Dad moved to Blue Lake. There's a massive speed bump right outside of this street labeled *Hope*. I wanted to take it when we were on bikes, but Dad wouldn't let us. Then, when Brian and I went, we wanted to check it out, but on each side of the street were these burly bouncer type guys trying—but failing—to fit in. I have no doubt they'd have stopped us. Then Brian got the call to fill in for the Sunday morning news, and I haven't been back since. And tons of people walk down that street, Lara. I just don't think we're the *right* people allowed to go there, too."

"But what makes a person the *right* person?"

"I have no idea."

"There you go. Much better."

I look in the bathroom mirror. My eyes are swollen and puffy. A large bruise covers my left cheek where I'd hit the pavement. The doctor had said I'd been lucky I didn't crack my cheekbone. My left arm is sore and also bruised. My hair hangs straight where Lara combed it out. I touch the spot where doctors had shaved part of the top of my head for stitches. It's tender.

"It will heal. Everything's going to be okay. And your hair will grow back." Lara hugs me lightly. "Plus, now you have Auggie, the farting dog, to keep you company.

"You named him Auggie?"

"Nope! *Nolan* named him Auggie!" She pulls out her bag and hands me Brian's gift to Nolan. She pushes the button. Auggie waddles his legs in the air before making a farting noise.

"Brilliant. Now all of my dreams have come true."

Chapter 24

"Linda isn't going to like this very much," I say to Brian as he unlocks my apartment door. "She doesn't like change."

"Linda is going to have to learn to deal with it. I'm not going to compete with a *cat* for your affections."

I smile. "Are you sure the allergy shot will work?"

"I guess we'll find out. Still have that EpiPen?"

"That's not even a little bit funny."

"I'm sorry. Yes, the doctor assured me I'd be fine for around a month. And then, if you still like me, I'll have to get another shot."

"You really don't need to do this. I am completely fine staying alone. I'm not a little girl. I know I'll be safe. I have good neighbors—and Linda."

"I have no doubt that Linda would win in a fight. Of course you are fine. You're doing this for *me. I* need to make sure you're sleeping and eating and all of those things. I'd go crazy if I couldn't see that for myself."

Brian leads me to the bedroom which is a disaster. I hadn't been expecting company when I left for work three days ago. Thank goodness the neighbor has a key and had been able to feed Linda.

As soon as I'm in bed, Linda jumps onto my chest. "Hey, girl. Nice to see you, too." She rubs her head against my chin. "Sorry about the mess."

"I guess there are still things I need to learn about you, like that you are a total slob. He shakes his head back and forth in total judgment as he picks up dirty clothes from around the room and deposits then into an empty basket mere feet away.

"I'm not a slob. I'm busy. I have more important things to do than clean."

"Like read erotic fiction?" He holds up a romance book with a bare-chested man on the cover.

"That is *not* erotic fiction!"

"Uh-huh. Like I believe you."

"You're hopeless."

"That reminds me. What about we take another trip back to Blue Lake when you feel better? See if we can get down Hope Street?"

"That would be a great idea, but you didn't tell me what Jerry said when you told him…"

"that I'm madly in love with you—or just *mad?*" He laughs before plopping down on the bed next to me. Linda runs out of the bedroom door.

"Something like that."

"He said he already knew. He said *everybody* knew."

"But how?"

"I guess we ooze hormones when we're around each other?" He throws up his hands.

"That is gross. Don't talk like that." I sink lower onto my pillow.

"Are you comfortable?" he asks affectionately, tucking a blanket over my chest.

"With you here I am, but you can't stay, Brian. You have to work this week. You need to go home."

"Nope. I packed enough to stay for a few days, at least at night. Plus, there are dry cleaners in Brookfield, too. And you can wash my underwear, so I'm good to go."

"We're at the *I'm washing your underwear* stage now?"

"I'd like us to be." Brian leans over and kisses me softly on the lips.

"You're pretty confident."

"Not always. I was terrified when Jerry called. I couldn't imagine losing you when I'd just met you. There's so much more I want to know about you, so much more I want to do with you—in and out of this bed." He winks.

"Barf! Just when I think you're being sweet." I shake my head.

"I'm only playing. But seriously, I want to be with you, to see things and do things in Chicago, on trips, in Arizona."

"Does that mean you're asking me to be your *girlfriend?*" I giggle when I say it out loud.

"Aww, it's like we're sixteen."

"I don't think I would have liked you when you were sixteen."

"Probably not. I was only prom king *twice!*"

"How can you be prom king twice?"

"I told you I moved around a lot. Let's just say my popularity and charm caught on quickly when I moved after being knighted at one school and being chosen again three weeks later at my new school."

"You must have been incorrigible to live with!"

"Ha! Yes, I was horrible."

"You wouldn't have liked me, either," I say.

"I doubt that."

"Nope. I was chess club captain and yearbook editor. I hated the prom king."

"I'm glad we found each other now. That's what matters most." He kisses me again. "Now get some sleep. I'm going to set up a workstation on your kitchen table if I can find some space."

"Yeah, good luck with that."

"Do I need to do anything with that four-legged beast?"

"Please. Give her a one third cup of dry food. It's in the pantry in the kitchen. Thank you."

"You're welcome. Night. Night."

"Wait! There's something I want you to know—something I didn't tell you before."

"Know what?" he asks, not breaking eye contact.

"I love you, too."

"I know you do," he says, smiling.

And I sleep better than I have in days.

Chapter 25

"Meg Popkin is recovering well at home after falling victim to a gang mugging on the 'L' platform a week ago. After leaving work, she was brutally attacked with a golf club. She was left for dead on the pavement and had her belongings stolen mere blocks from the station where she works. We have Meg on the screen now. Meg, first of all, how are you doing?" Jessalyn Bowers asks from the WDOU news desk.

I'd picked out a pretty yellow blouse for the interview. I had Brian clasp the heart-shaped locket I wore that Dad had given me with Mom's picture for my birthday the year she died. I'm on camera all the time, but it's different when I'm being interviewed instead of asking the questions. Plus, Jessalyn Bowers is the absolute last person in the world that I'd want to host this interview, but I wasn't given a choice. *Ratings* Jerry had said. *Ratings. Taking one for the team.* I glance at Brian who gives me a thumbs-up off-camera. "Hello, Jessalyn. I'm doing well, thank you. I miss everyone at the station."

"We miss you, too, Meg. Tell us. What do you remember about that night?"

I take a slow breath and smile fakely so that Jessalyn does not know how rattled my mind is at this moment. "Sorry, Jessalyn. I really don't remember what happened. I guess that's a good thing, right?"

"I suppose so. Tell us about the injuries you incurred. It must have been *awful*," she says sickeningly fake.

"I had a lot of bruises and headaches from the gash in my head."

"Oh? A *gash?* That sounds serious. Did you need surgery?"

"No, just stitches. My care team at Cook County Hospital was great…" I look at Brian, "as is my care team at home."

"Hmm," says Jessalyn.

Knowing that I've shaken her feels too good.

"Tell us, Meg, what are the next steps in your recovery?"

"I need to have the stitches in my head removed. Otherwise, my bruising is healing nicely. I'm being well cared for," I remind her again.

"That's great news. We're following your case in the court system. A security camera caught the attack live, and we will be playing it for the first time tonight in hopes that someone will recognize the perpetrators."

"Camera?" I don't understand. No one told me anything about camera evidence of my attack. And they're going to play the tape on the news? This can't be happening.

"Yes, Meg. Take a look."

Jessalyn pivots to the video. I can't see it, but I can hear my voice—my pleadings, *Stop! Stop! Don't hurt me. Please!* and then silence from me and laughter from others. *Wallet. Phone. Damn, she's got a lot of crap in here.*

"Please take a careful look at the close-up pictures we pulled from this video. If you have any information about this case, please call the Chicago Police Department tip hotline at 555-345-4597. The video is also available on our website." She turns her attention back to me. "Thanks again for joining us tonight, Meg. We look forward to seeing you soon."

"Thanks, Jessalyn." *Thanks for nothing* I want to say.

"What the hell was that?" I can hear Brian yelling on the phone. "She's traumatized by that night, and you ambush her like that? I don't care if it makes good television. Meg is your *co-worker*. Doesn't that mean anything to you? Shut up, Jessa." Then he throws his phone on the couch. He almost hits Linda which doesn't help their relationship bonding.

Then my phone—my new phone—dings. "It's Jerry."

"What's *he* got to say for himself?" Brian asks.

I've never seen Brian this mad before.

"He said he didn't know," I say, reading Jerry's text.

"I'm not one hundred percent sure I believe him, but I sure as hell don't trust Jessa."

"What did you do to her?" I ask. "Cause whatever it is, I think she's taking it out on me."

"I didn't do anything to her. That was the problem. She *wanted* me to do something to her, but I refused. She's not my type. She's arrogant and superficial, only a pretty face as far as I can tell. And she's worried."

"Worried about what?" I ask. "Surely not worried about the crime on the streets of Chicago and catching my attackers."

"That was a dick move. I'm sorry you had to hear that."

"I suppose it was going to happen sooner or later though I didn't expect to have to react live in front of thousands of people the first time I heard it."

Brian kisses me and pulls me close to him. "She's worried that you're going to take her job when I take the anchor seat away from Steve."

"I don't *want* the anchor job. You know that. I want to tell feature stories, write my own stories."

"She doesn't know that. Let's let her worry a bit longer."

"And why do you think I'd get her job anyway if you got Steve's job?"

"Because we're a duo, Meg. Can't you see it: *Chicago lovers sell the news. Tune in weeknights at 6:00 and 10:00.*"

I roll my eyes as I kiss him back. "I can barely stand you in my apartment every night. How could I stand working so closely with you every night at work, too?"

He raises one eyebrow, a cute talent I've learned to recognize this week. "Prove you're tired of having me here."

"Okay?"

"I'm going to go into your bedroom, kick Linda out, take off my shirt…"

"Uh-huh."

"Take off my belt."

"Uh-huh."

"Take off my pants."

"Interesting."

"Take off my underwear—the red ones, by the way."

"Okay."

"And I'm going to lie on top of your bed. *Naked*."

"Yes?"

"And I'll see if it's true that you can't stand having me in your apartment every night."

I watch Brian walk to my bedroom, shaking his hips for emphasis. I can't help but laugh. And I can't help but follow. Bluff called. Brian's going to score.

Chapter 26

I'm going back to work on Wednesday. I've been home for two weeks, and I'm ready to return to civilization. Spending so much time alone has sucked the life out of everyday joys that used to make me happy like sipping my first morning coffee or watching reruns of Sex and the City or doing yoga. Now, some mornings, the only thing that gets me out of bed is Linda's incessant meowing and pawing at my face to feed her.

My stitches are out, and my bruises have faded. The only scar that remains is on the inside of my brain that reacts to every loud noise or unexpected person walking by. I'd had my first nightmare the night after I send Brian back to his place to tend to his own business. Someone was holding me down and striking me over and over in the stomach, and every time I yelled *no!* I got hit again. I woke up in a sweat. Only finding Linda in her usual sleeping spot on her cat bed on the couch and shutting her in the bedroom so she'd had to sleep with me allowed me to fall asleep again. Three nights later I dreamed that someone dressed in all black kept pulling my hat off, and every time I reached for it back, they'd lure me closer to the train tracks until I finally fell on them. I only woke up when the train lights approached. I have my second virtual therapy session tonight. Talking about my fears with a complete stranger is actually a lot better than it sounds.

Brian and I are driving to Blue Lake for the weekend. Everyone and their uncle travels to their summer homes in Michigan on Friday nights, so we're trying to get out of town early Saturday morning. I give Linda an extra feeding, so she will forgive me for leaving her. She's gotten very used to having me here every day. Whom am I fooling, though? She'll sleep every day and eagerly eat her dinner at night when the neighbor stops by.

"Mind if I drive?" Brian asks when I pull up to the no parking zone in front of his building and roll down the window. He's carrying the same duffle bag he uses when he stays over.

"Actually, I'd be grateful if you drove. I've got a killer headache."

"I thought they were getting better."

"I'm way better. Don't worry." I kiss him on the cheek, and since I'm not good company for conversation we listen to an Office Ladies podcast episode—the recap of the dinner party episode where Michael and Jan have a horrible fight in front of their guests. It's cringey perfect.

Dad hugs me for at least a full minute before letting go. "You look tired. Do you want to lie down?" he asks.

"I'm not tired, Dad. Honest. I'd love to walk around to tell you the truth. Fresh air and quiet small town noises are the prescriptions I need."

"Okay, um…" He looks us up and down.

I hold up my wrist. "Got my blue bracelet, Dad."

"And I've got my Cubs hat," Brian says, pointing to his head.

Dad blinks his eyes a couple of times as if he's satisfied without even acknowledging that we've tipped our cards to knowing about this weird Blue Lake color identification thing. He's wearing red shorts.

We walk to Rosie's Restaurant where I order a BLT sandwich. Dad and Brian share meals—a buffalo burger and grilled chicken sandwich. I dip into their fries as Dad doesn't eat very much. In fact, Brian almost eats the entirety of both meals. I remember what Lara said about Dad at Nolan's birthday party.

I put my hand atop Dad's. It's old and leathery, a life of hard work well-lived. "How are you feeling, Dad?"

"Great, just great," he says too enthusiastically.

I'm not sure if I believe him, but there is no sense in questioning further. Brian pays the check which I think is sweet. Then we walk to the lake, Dad's arm looped through mine to steady him.

"Don't bring up the kayaks," I whisper to Brian who stands on my other side. "We don't want to raise too much suspicion today."

"Got it, Chief." He kisses me on the cheek and grabs hold of my free hand.

Dad picks out a picnic table with a pretty view of the lake which is glistening like a thousand twinkling stars today. It's hot—nearly 90 degrees—but when you have winters like we do in the Midwest, it's hard to justify complaining about the weather when you get such a bright sunny day. Plus, there's an easterly breeze that is refreshing.

"I brought dessert," says Dad. He reaches into a red bag he's been carrying and pulls out a plastic container. He sets it on the table and removes the lid.

"Cupcakes?" I ask. "When did you learn to cook?" I raise my eyebrows in surprise. Dad's only foray into cooking had been on the grill and even *that* didn't always end well. Lara chipped a front tooth on a piece of steak in high school, right before Homecoming. She was mortified and did *not* appreciate it when I started calling her Chippy.

"There are so many things we can do here in Blue Lake, things to learn. I took a cooking class, well, a baking class. With your birthday coming up next week, I wanted to surprise you."

"You have a *birthday* next week?" Brian looks at me, his mouth hanging open in surprise.

I guess we haven't gotten all of the basic *getting to know you* boyfriend/girlfriend things off our list yet. "It's Friday, but it's no big deal."

"What? It is a huge deal. You're turning 30! That's a milestone birthday, Meg!" Dad is a little too excited.

Brian smiles wider than a slice of watermelon on the Fourth of July which happens to be this week, too. "I knew I was dating an old woman. I knew it!"

I sock him in the stomach playfully. "I am *not* old!"

"Well, you're older than me."

"By how much, Brian?" asks Dad.

"By a whole year, Paul. Meg's really robbing the cradle."

They share a hearty laugh at my expense. "While you two goons guffaw, I'm going to try one of Dad's

214

cupcakes." I sink my teeth into the yellow cake with chocolate frosting. Mom always made a huge deal about our birthdays. She'd bake some sort of shaped cake depending upon our interests at the time of our birthday. I've had cakes with everything from Strawberry Shortcake to Barbie to Mickey Mouse, even a poorly executed cake shaped like Nick Jonas from the Jonas Brothers. It's a sweet memory, and I appreciate what my dad is trying to do. "It's delicious, Dad. Thanks." I give him a hug mid-bite of his own cupcake.

"How often do you come to the lake?" Brian asks, licking his fingers less than gracefully.

"The lake? I come to Blue Lake every day, at least I go to…" He clears his throat which leads to a coughing fit. "Excuse me. Sorry about that."

I give him a bottle of water. "Are you okay?"

"Yes, yes. I'm fine. I've got a bit of cake stuck in my throat."

"You were getting ready to tell us where you go every day—on the lake?" I ask, not willing to let this moment pass.

"I come to the lake every day, that's all. Sometimes I sit down here. Sometimes I sit on the deck of the library with a good book. It's quite a beautiful asset."

"She sure is beautiful," Brian agrees as he stares out over the lake, full of kayaks and rowboats moving back and forth.

Dad laughs. "Are you talking about Blue Lake or my daughter?"

Brian's entire face lights up. "I think you know the answer to that question, Mr. Popkin." He caresses my face and kisses my cheek. "Just helping you out with this bit of frosting," he says and kisses me again.

"Okay, lovebirds, let's get back to the condo. Do you kids mind helping me install the new kitchen hardware I bought for my cabinets?"

"We'd love to help."

Dad falls asleep in his chair mid-way through our home improvement project. He sits in a comfortable chair that faces the lake. Brian and I finish installing the new kitchen cabinet knobs as we listen to him snore.

"Your dad seems pretty peaceful right now," says Brian as he pops the top off the beer bottle I've handed to him.

"Do you believe that in the almost thirty years I've known my father, I have never seen him nap?"

"Seriously? My dad fell asleep every Sunday afternoon at 1:00 when the first football game of the day would start. He'd wake up by halftime, swear that he'd seen the whole game, and proceed to eat a bag of microwave popcorn—like clockwork. It was amazing! But don't worry," he says, patting my leg. "He's in his 60s. People get tired as they age. He's been playing tour guide all day. Give the man a break."

"I suppose you're right."

"Should we sneak out to Hope Street now while we can?"

"No." I shake my head. "We need to wait until late tonight, when the security beefs won't be out reading or pruning imaginary trees, hopefully."

"Then maybe *you* should take a nap if we're going to be out late." He looks at me with such concern.

"I think you're right. Want to join me?"

Brian shakes his head *no* adamantly. "No way. I don't trust myself, and even some boundaries *I* won't cross like banging my girlfriend in her father's home."

"*Banging?* You're incurable. See you in a bit." I kiss him on the lips with a tiny bite before I pull away.

"Ouch! What was that?"

"Punishment for your silliness."

"Hmm...I'll try to be naughty more often then." He giggles like a schoolboy.

"Night-night, Brian."

Chapter 27

"Hearts are trump," I yell as I throw a ten of hearts onto the table. Dad and I are partnering against Brian and Sandra, an older woman who wears a wig, laughs at everything Brian says, and swears like a truck driver in a heated game of euchre. Sandra and Brian are winning, but the tide is about to turn.

Dad and Sandra are dressed alike—sort of. Dad wears a nice red Polo shirt while Sandra sports a bright red necklace. Brian hasn't taken off his Cubs hat since we've arrived, and I've decided to wear a blue short-sleeve t-shirt along with my blue *M* bracelet. That way there's no confusion or embarrassment for Dad's friends that we don't *belong*.

"Sandra, how long have you lived in Blue Lake?" Brian asks, Mr. Reporter turning up the heat.

"Me? Oh, I ain't been here long. But it's the best decision I done made." She smiles at my dad. "Lots of goodness here. Right, Paul? Tell your daughter and her husband."

"Boyfriend!" I say.

"For now," she says under her breath. "Tell your family how cool it is here, Paul." Dad nods in agreement. "Didn't know such a place existed."

Dad clears his throat. He starts tapping his index finger on the table. "Spades!" he yells, a little too loudly.

"What do you mean by that? That *you didn't know such a place existed?*"

She shoots a frightened look at Dad, knowing she's already said too much. I'm not getting that answer.

After Dad and I lose a second game, we say goodbye to Sandra and ride back up the elevator. "It's late, kids. Do you mind if I turn in for the evening? I'm exhausted."

I raise my eyebrows at Brian as if to say *doesn't he remember the two-hour nap he had this afternoon?*

"No problem, Paul. It's been a full day. Meg and I will take advantage of that pretty view of Blue Lake out on the balcony and then turn in ourselves. We have a long drive tomorrow."

"Sounds good. Thanks for visiting, kids. I always enjoy my family. I told you this would be good for the family, right Meg?"

"I don't unders…"

"Yes, it's been a great decision, Paul. See you in the morning." Brian winks at me and puts a finger to his lips.

He's right, of course, Dad won't give me the answers I want, so there's no use in riling him up.

Brian and I wait until Dad is sound asleep, his snores flowing out a sketchy tune from his bedroom. "Did you bring a red shirt?" I ask.

"Yep. Got it. Do you have yours?"

"Yes. Let's change. But be quiet!"

We tiptoe into the guestroom. "You look good in red," says Brian. "It compliments your hair well."

"Uh, thanks. But we don't have time for this right now."

"Are you sure?" He pulls me in close, and I inhale his cologne.

"Did you have to reapply before our mission?" I giggle. "You know what your cologne does to me."

"And *that's* why I reapplied."

"You are crazy. Come on. We have work to do." I kiss him on the cheek and pinch him on the butt before we race each other down the stairs of the condo building.

There aren't many people out and about in Blue Lake at this time of night—almost midnight. The town is well lit, though. Streetlights line the streets illuminating the small stores and restaurants below them. There are lights around Blue Lake, too, shining a spotlight on the perfectly still water that rests as well as the residents of its namesake. The people that still walk about seem to be coming from a bar south of town between the Blue Lake Hub and Hope Street. It dawns on me that I haven't seen what the other residences look like in Blue Lake as the areas around Dad's building are commercial or community resources like the library. "Maybe we should get to Hope Street the back way," I say to Brian in a whisper though no one is near enough to hear us.

"What back way?"

"Well, there's no sign that said *Dead End* so there must be another way in. There's got to be a neighborhood or something on that part of the town that we haven't seen yet."

"Sounds like a good idea to me. Lead the way."

"Let me check my phone." I open Google Maps and zoom in on the area of Blue Lake. But it doesn't exist—not *this* Blue Lake, of course.

"What's wrong?" Brian asks, my face twisted in confusion.

"Blue Lake is not on the map."

"I don't understand."

"I do," I say, the clarity forming in my mind. "It's another piece of the puzzle. Remember the sign? It's a *cooperative community*. And whatever that means, Google doesn't recognize *this* Blue Lake as a town."

"Holy Shit!" says Brian a bit too loud.

"We still have to get to Hope Street. Let's see if there's a back way in through that neighborhood over there." I point to a row of neatly placed homes.

"Come on. We're wasting time," says Brian. He grabs my hand and leads me past city hall and under security cameras mounted on the side of the building. We slip quietly by until we see a sign marked *Paradise Row*.

"That street runs parallel to Hope Street," I say. We start running as we get closer.

"Crap! What was that?" I ask as Brian and I cross under the street sign for Paradise Row. A red light like a laser shoots out from the top of the sign and crosses over the sidewalk when we pass its shadow.

Brian grabs my arm and pulls me behind a bush in the yard of the house closest to the sidewalk. "It's got to be some kind of weird security measure. The residents of Blue Lake do *not* want anyone on this street, either."

"At least the ones that don't belong here," I add. "What do we do now?" I put my hand on my chest to slow my heartbeat.

"Let's get as far away from the street as possible." We run behind trees, bushes, and sheds, jumping from house to house as we make our way down the block through backyards.

"Damn! They have a motion sensor," I say after we run behind a pair of evergreen trees in at least the fourth or fifth backyard.

"Who's out there?" an elderly woman yells. "Is someone out there?" she repeats.

We freeze. Brian pulls me tightly to his chest so we appear as if part of the trunk of the tree. After what seems like an hour, but is likely no more than a minute, we drop to our knees and crawl into the next yard when the woman returns inside. "Brian, what the hell is going on?"

"I don't know, but we aren't going back now without at least *some* answers."

We continue to run in a crouched down position hoping that works to avert motion detectors, and we stay as far away from the houses as possible. Each house appears like the one before—same size, same color, as if they'd all been built in an assembly line fashion in a period of weeks.

"Ouch!" Brian says too loudly for the circumstances. He tumbles forward onto the grass.

"What happened?" I crawl over to him. He sits up and rubs his shin.

"I knocked into something—didn't see it. It hurt like a truck rammed into my shin!"

I turn the spotlight of my phone to the low setting and shine it in the direction we'd come from. "It's a fountain," I say. "Not a truck." He can't see my small smile.

"Like a water fountain?" Brian asks as he rubs his leg.

"Not like a water fountain from the halls of high school but like a water fountain feature people put in their yards for decoration."

"Let me see. Shine the light again, please."

I shine the light on the water fountain, a fish mouth spitting water into a large bowl and cycling back to the fish's mouth.

"I mean, it's pretty, but why would someone keep a fountain so far away from their house when they can't even see it?" Brian asks.

"I have no idea, but it's not the first fountain I've seen tonight. A few houses back there were wine bottles dripping water into a rectangle container. I thought it was cool though it wasn't exactly the time to point it out to you." I dip my hand into the fish fountain water. "The water is a bit cool but nothing remarkable. It's just water." I check the time on my phone. It's 1:00 a.m. "Brian, it's taken almost an hour to get a few blocks. We have to keep going. Can you walk…or at least crawl?"

"If you can do this with bruises all over your body, I can do this with one little bruise on my shin. But hang on." He sprinkles water from the fountain on his shin. "There—all better now. I'm cured. Bruise is gone." He smiles, and even in the dimness of the backyards, it lights up his face.

"If only it were that easy. Let's go."

Now we see the fountains everywhere. We can't miss them now that we know what we are looking for: a lion's head fountain, a fountain made from a child's toy car, large flower pots set up for water to flow like a waterfall from one pot to the next. They are actually quite beautiful in both their simplicity and their designs.

"Only one more yard to go!" Brian grabs my hand, and we run faster, defying the motion detectors that might be near, too close to be stopped now.

Brian looks at me. I look at him, wide-eyed. Below us stands a woman howling into the night at the base of a small waterfall. "What the hell?" we say at the same time.

Chapter 28

We lie on our stomachs which hurts more than I'd like to admit. The woman is dressed in all red, a dress that clings to her body from the strong flowing water. Her arms outstretched, she yells—not anything we can understand—more like the guttural yells of a woman in labor—at least it reminds me of Lara during the birth of Nolan, since I'd been the only one with her when he arrived early in her bathroom at home. The water above the woman's head flows directly over her body, but the pool she stands in appears to also be fed from two smaller waterfalls that meet up, the water no more than a few feet deep.

The woman is not alone. A man—younger than the woman by looks—is sitting with his legs crossed in the pool to her right, the one closest to us. He appears to be praying or meditating. He is quiet and does not seem irritated by the woman's continued cries.

Brian and I just stare, absorbed in our own thoughts, trying to process what we are seeing. Suddenly, red lights, like the one we'd seen at the stop sign, flash over the waterfalls, highlighting the water and making it appear red. The woman scampers quickly over rocks that jut out from the waterfall's pool. The man follows, his eyes scoping the horizon of the waterfalls looking for something. They each grab towels from the grass nearby and run away without ever speaking to each other.

"What's happening?" Brian asks.

"I don't...I don't know. Brian, I'm scared." I watch the red lights continue to flash over the waterfalls while I lie still. Brian and I look at each other as a new light, a bright flashlight beam, rests on us.

"Get up slowly," we hear from somewhere in the yard behind us.

We do as we are told. Brian grabs my hand and pulls me closer. He puts his other hand in the air. "Hey, man. Sorry. We wanted to see the waterfalls. We don't mean any harm."

"We...we wanted to see the falls at night...because...because they're so pretty. And it was worth it. They are stunning." I try not to sound nervous, but I am not fooling anyone.

"You're trespassing." A man around the age of my dad walks closer to us. He's fully dressed, not in pajamas as you'd assume in the middle of the night. His face is highlighted by a full beard, and I think he's the first person I've met in Blue Lake who doesn't smile.

"We are really sorry," says Brian. "We will get off your land right away."

"Why didn't you walk down the street like everyone else does? It's clearly marked." The man looks at our clothing—red shirts, part of the club—trying to understand.

"Lover's spat," I say. "My boyfriend wanted to go down Hope Street, but I wanted to try something different. I won."

"You know, happy wife, happy life?" Brian shrugs his shoulders and grins goofily.

"She said *boyfriend*."

"Huh?"

"Oh, that's another argument brewing. He *wants* me to be his wife, but I'm not ready."

"There aren't many couples in Blue Lake," the man says as he walks closer to Brian. "Usually people move here alone."

"Yes, well, that's true," I stammer.

"What ails you?" he asks so close now that I could bop him on the nose.

"Ails me?" Brian repeats.

"You know what I mean. What brings you to Blue Lake? I have cancer in my pancreas. Been living here for six months now, four months longer than I was supposed to be alive."

Shocks of understanding hit my brain. "Well, we both—we both have, uh…the bruises. We both have the bruises," I say confidently now. I point to my arm and the side of my face where if you look closely you can still see the outlines of the bruises from my fall on the train platform. The man looks carefully, not convinced. "And here," I point to the top of my head. "My hair is finally growing back after the…uh…the tumor was removed."

"Aw, yes, I see," he says. "What about you?" He looks at Brian, still not smiling.

"I have some—the bruises—too. He points to his shin which is already glowing a deep purple after his run-in with the fish water fountain.

"I believe you. But don't come out here again—this way at least. The security team is going to be all over this situation with you setting off the flashing lights."

"Okay. We, uh, but…well…why exactly did the lights start flashing" Brian asks.

231

"Because there's only one way to the falls—Hope Street down there." He points to the street below. "Up here people have the water from the falls in their yard fountains. We use that water when we're hurting bad. Otherwise, we have to travel back down Paradise Row and get to Hope Street just like everyone else. We aren't special up here."

"We understand. We're still new here. Real sorry, sir. Do you *have* to tell security?" I ask.

"I don't have to, no," he says.

"Thank you so much," I say. "We are really grateful and don't want to make any trouble."

"I don't have to 'cause it's already done."

Chapter 29

"What do we do now?" I yell at Brian after the man walks back into his house.

"I don't know. I don't know. Think. Think. *Think*. We can't go back on Paradise Row because the red laser lights will go off again, like the one by the stop sign. *They*—whoever the hell that is—will likely be waiting for us at the end of Hope Street if we go down the hill to the street."

"Well, we can't evaporate into thin air!" I say.

"Or can we?"

"What are you talking about?" I'm tired. My head hurts. And I don't want to hurt my dad. Somehow this is going to hurt my dad. And he's so happy now. Why couldn't I let him be happy? Why do I always have to know *why*?

Brian grabs my shoulders, a little too hard. "I've got it, Meg!"

"Ouch."

"Oh, sorry! Meg, you must be so tired."

"What are we going to do?" I feel like crying.

He points to Hope Street which ends at the waterfalls. "We wait."

"Huh?"

233

"The lights are still flashing, so we wouldn't be setting them off again. No one knows what we look like except for the man who chewed us out. We can slide down the hill, hide out under those bushes over there." He points to three tall bushes that line the edge of the pool that collects the water from the waterfall. "And come morning, we'll wade into the waterfall like everyone else that comes here. We'll be wet when we leave. We'll leave alone, so they won't be able to spot that *trouble-making couple,* or whatever they've labeled us."

"But what about Dad? He will worry when we aren't there in the morning, which is only a few hours from now. Oh, man, I have messed so much up." I'm so tired I feel delirium setting in, and I want to scream at the top of my lungs like the woman in the red dress.

Brian tips up my chin and puts his face close to mine. "You haven't screwed anything up. You love your dad. You want to know what's going on in this town that took him away from his family. And, if I know you correctly, which I think I do, you didn't make your bed after your nap, so he'll think we got up early for a coffee run or a run *run.*"

"You're right. I didn't make the bed. I love you so much right now, Brian Welter."

"And I love you, Meggin Popkin. Now let's make a bed under a bush."

A few hours later as the sun rises over Blue Lake, the first people of the day travel down Hope Street to the waterfalls. They walk in fully clothed, mostly quiet. Perhaps those that want to yell come in the middle of the night like the woman in the red dress. Brian goes to the falls first. He joins a young man with no hair who is sitting under the water washing over him so peacefully. Brian sits under the waterfall nearest the bush. He closes his eyes. I wonder if he is praying. I wonder if Brian prays at all. After a few minutes he stands up, shakes his body to remove the excess water, and walks to Hope Street—and *hopefully* to a safe trek back to Dad's condo.

After I can no longer see him, I step out from behind the bush. No one sees me, everyone lost in their own thoughts, their own rituals. I walk toward the water, careful not to fall on the rocks that make a sort of path through the water. An old woman wobbles unsteadily away from the main waterfall. I step into her place under the water. I tip my head back and let the water wash over me, wetting every inch of my body. It's slightly warm as the sun already shines brightly. I do say a prayer, for Dad, for Lara, the boys, Rick, a prayer for Brian, and me, and maybe even for *Brian and me*. I've not been a particularly spiritual person, but when the power moves you, you move with it. And I feel that power as I stand under this waterfall. Is that what everyone experiences here? A line is forming as I step upon Hope Street. I pass people waiting quietly for their turn under the waterfalls—what I can only imagine they believe holds some sort of healing power. I think back over the many people I've met in Blue Lake, many with thinning hair or coughs or bandages. I can't be the one to tell them it's not real. They won't listen to me. Their minds are made up. But why is Dad here? Why is *he* in Blue Lake?

As I near the end of Hope Street and see the connecting road with bicyclists already out for their morning trip around the lake, I try to stay in the middle so that I don't attract attention from either side. A man had held out a towel for me as I exited the water. I don't know if he had an extra or if that was his job, but I'm grateful. I use the towel to hide my face as I attempt to dry my hair. I see the bouncers, the security twins. They aren't at their posts, though. They are picking up some sort of trash that is littered along the street. I use the opportunity to slip past them. I have to try with all my might not to run the rest of the way back to the condo.

"Hey!" Brian yells before I enter the Blue Lake Hub. "Did you have any problems?" He crosses the street from outside a drug store. He hands me a bottle of water.

"Thank you. I needed that." I take a long drink of water. "No problems, shockingly. The bouncers were picking up trash. Weird."

Brian chuckles. "Awesome. I was hoping they'd get curious."

"What do you mean?" I take another drink.

"I didn't want them stopping you and giving you any trouble, so I reached into my pockets and started dropping trash along the street. I figured the condoms would make them curious."

"Excuse me—*condoms?*"

"Yeah, I had a few in my pocket," he grins sheepishly. "What can I say...I'm a believer in safety?" He laughs. "A guy's gotta do what a guy's gotta do. It worked, didn't it?"

"You are crazy."

"And smart. Don't forget smart."

"You're smart—or a smart ass." I take a slow breath. "Let's get our stories straight before we see Dad. Then we need to leave. I can't take any chances that bearded guy won't rat us out."

Dad isn't in the condo when we get upstairs. There's a note on the kitchen island.

Got called out. Will be back as soon as I can.
Love, Dad

"That's not good," says Brian, his eyes wide with concern.

"We need to go. *Now*. I'm too tired and sore and overwhelmed to process all of this, but I don't have a good feeling. We should leave."

"I agree. I'll drive. You can sleep all the way home."

"Are you awake enough to drive?"

"As soon as we get close enough to a *real* town again, I'll stop for coffee." He puts his hand on my shoulders and squeezes gently. It's the first time I've realized I'm holding so much tension.

"Let's go, Meg." He kisses the top of my head. We pack our clothes, make the bed, and lock the door behind us. We take the back stairs to the parking garage. I'm sad to not hug Dad goodbye, but something tells me he won't be sad that I'm gone.

Chapter 30

Brian was true to his word and let me sleep all the way home. We haven't even had time to process the past 24 hours. My head is splitting, and my body aches in new places. I'm supposed to go back to work on Wednesday, and I think I'll have to sleep for the next two days to be ready. Brian makes me a cup of tea in his condo before I drive back to Brookfield.

"So, what now?" he asks as he sits across from me with his own mug of tea.

"I don't know. It's clear that people in Blue Lake think there's some sort of healing power in those waterfalls. And that they don't want outsiders finding out."

"And that they've gone to pretty elaborate measures to keep people like us out. Flashing red lights?"

"Are we living in a sci-fi movie? I mean, it's ridiculous, right?" I ask.

"Pretty damn nuts. What are you going to do about your dad?"

"I don't know. I'm going to wait, I guess. I'll let him make the next move, tell me what he knows about what we did—if he knows—how much I screwed up his chance at happiness, whatever that means."

Brian sets down his mug and gets up from the kitchen stool. He wraps his arms around me. "It's going to work out, Meg. You'll see."

I call Lara on the way back to Brookfield for two reasons, one—to stay awake because every ounce of me is screaming to shut my eyes, and two—to fill her in on everything that happened while Brian and I were in Blue Lake. She's quieter than I've ever heard her be on the other end of a phone call. I get it. What can you say about something as crazy as what's happened today?

There is a message on my phone from Dad when I get home—three messages, actually. They are all vague. Things like: *Sorry I missed you. Call me.* I don't want to call him yet, though. How can one ever be ready for a chewing out from their own father? So, instead, I feed Linda, strip off my clothes, put on pajamas, and crawl into bed. Linda settles on top of the blankets after she's forgiven me with a full belly. And I sleep.

It's Monday morning when I wake up. I check the clock. I've been sleeping for fourteen hours. I don't want to stop either, not because my body still needs sleep, but because I don't want to face the day or anyone else. I've hurt my dad. I've disappointed my boss because I haven't given him a new feature story idea. I've let down the city because I became another crime statistic who couldn't give the police any information to help them put those criminals away so that they stop terrorizing innocent women like me. My head is spinning.

But Linda has other ideas. She is furious—hangry mad. Every time I roll over, she nips me—on the arm, on my shoulder. I throw the covers off in a sign of defeat, and she goes flying to the end of the bed.

After feeding Linda, I text Brian that I'm back in the land of the living. He's working and busy for the day. I decide to use my last days of sick leave to work from home. I *have* to find a story I can connect with that will please Jerry again, or I'm going to have to accept that I'll always be a common street reporter. It's an important job that's sustained me for almost seven years, but it's not enough anymore. Linda jumps on my lap. I navigate over her and open my laptop. There are a couple of new email messages related to the hospice story. It's shocking to me that so many people are still seeing this story, but that's the way social media works. One of the messages is from Spencer with a note about Robin, the patient whose brother Darrel

I had interviewed for the story. She had passed quietly in her sleep the night before surrounded by Darrel and her parents, another chapter closed with peace and dignity. Reading that email triggered a memory I'd forgotten about. When I'd told Spencer that Dad had moved to Michigan, he'd guessed Blue Lake right away. I'd never even heard of the town before. How had he? And why did he guess Blue Lake?

I punch in the numbers on my phone to Pine Crest and ask Hannah to transfer me to Spencer's office.

"Meg, you have been on my mind. How are you feeling?"

"Hi, Spencer. I'm much better now. Thanks. Going back to work on Wednesday."

"Ah, I imagine you've missed the job."

"Yes and no," I say honestly. "Thanks for the email about Robin."

"You're welcome. Darrel insisted that I let you know."

"That's very thoughtful. Listen, Spencer, I've been thinking about something you said when you asked me about Dad once during a visit for the news story."

"Yes?"

"When I mentioned that he had moved to Michigan and we weren't really sure why, you guessed that he'd moved to Blue Lake."

"How...how did you know that?"

Spencer is quiet on the other end of the line.

"Spencer? Are you still there?"

"Yes, Meg. Have you asked your dad why he moved to Blue Lake?"

"Yes, of course. He gave vague answers. He told me to trust him, that this was going to be good for the family which I still don't understand."

Spencer is quiet again. "I don't think it's my place to answer that question."

I can't hold back with proper politeness. "There's something weird going on in Blue Lake. The residents all wear red at least on some part of their body or carry something red, and guests have something blue. There's a street called Hope Street that has these mysterious waterfalls and..."

Spencer interrupts me. "Did your dad tell you about the waterfalls?"

"No, of course not, but Brian and I—*Brian Welter from the station*—saw them. We had to somersault our way there in the middle of the night, but we saw them. And we saw the people who came. Spencer, those people think that the waterfalls give them some sort of healing power or who knows what. And I don't understand. Why would people think that? And why does Dad live there? He's not dying." A lump rises to my throat, shaken free from the heaviness in my chest.

"Talk to him, Meg."

I bob my head up and down which I know he can't see. I can't keep avoiding my dad. "But Spencer, why did you guess Blue Lake?"

"Can I tell you something off the record?"

"Of course. I'm not reporting for a story."

"I had a patient about six months ago who came to Pine Crest to die peacefully. Her name was Abigail. One night Abigail's aging husband had gone home to get a few things, and I was doing my rounds when I noticed that she was alone. She called me to her bedside and said, *"Can I tell you a secret?"* I receive lots of end-of-life confessions kind of like a priest, so I told her that I'd be happy to hear whatever she wanted to say. She'd smiled and patted the bed for me to move closer. I sat in a chair and moved it as close to the bed as possible. Something about being so close gives people comfort that anything they say can't possibly leave the room. But I think you need to hear this story, Meg—off the record."

"Yes, please go on." My heart is nearly beating out of my chest.

"She said she'd lived in a wonderful place called Blue Lake, Michigan. She'd had to leave her husband to go there, but he'd been able to visit though never fully understanding why she'd felt the need to be there. In fact, he'd been really angry at first but believed her that it was best for their relationship and their kids and grandkids that she go for *"only a little while"* she'd said. She described the town so beautifully, the lovely lake—the town's namesake—and the friendliest people on the planet. She'd played games and had coffee and took walks and joined groups that interested her. And then she told me about the waterfalls."

"What did she say about the waterfalls?" I resist the urge to grab a notepad and start taking notes.

"She told me that there were waterfalls in town that had a healing power, that she visited them every day for six months. I can't do proper justice to the beautiful way she described what it felt like to stand under those waterfalls."

"But did it cure her? She died at Pine Crest, right?"

"Sadly, she did die here. But, Meg, she *lived* when she was at Blue Lake. She lived eight months longer than the time doctors gave her to live. And she lived well. She laughed and she enjoyed nature and she enjoyed hobbies and made new friends. She enjoyed her family when they'd visit. And she had *hope.*"

"Hope Street," I say out loud.

"Huh?"

"The waterfalls were on Hope Street."

"Oh, yes. You mentioned that."

"But I don't understand. She still died. The waterfalls don't contain magical powers or healing powers."

"Hope is a powerful medicine. Hope and positivity can do miraculous things for people that are sick."

"But surely the people in Blue Lake know that it can't last forever. That they can't ward off death?"

"I'm not sure what they think. Everyone is different, of course. But the hope that the community of Blue Lake promises is powerful. And if people choose to spend the last weeks, months, or years getting as much joy out of life as possible in a community whose premise is doing nothing more than providing joy and positivity and *hope*—well, I see nothing wrong with that, even if the waterfalls give them a false sense of healing."

"Then why did Abigail die here instead of in Blue Lake?"

"She missed her husband. And her health did decline. She'd told me that the health committee at Blue Lake had told her it was okay to return home."

"Health committee?"

"Blue Lake has a team of geriatric and oncology and other specialties of doctors who give medical advice and care to its residents. When care need exceeds their ability to be helpful, they encourage residents to find the next stop for their end of care life."

"So, Abigail and people like her figure out that Blue Lake is just a farce, some made up lie that their lives are going to be extended if they live there? Is it all about money?" I don't mean to yell but I do. "This doesn't make any sense."

"When people are told by doctors that they have a terminal illness, the process of acceptance can take time and is often painful. Blue Lake offers a buffer between the news of the diagnosis and the actual final days of a person's life. Plus, sometimes people *do* heal. There are such things as miracles, you know. And new treatments, new medicines. But often what I think happens is that the *quality* of life shifts for many who move to Blue Lake. It's that positivity and hope that I talked about. It really works. And when it stops working, well, usually by then people have softened to the understanding of what *terminal* means and can accept the result and see Blue Lake for what it was for them—an extension of life that gave them some of the best opportunities to live, to *really live* with joy. By the way, Abigail isn't the only patient I've talked to about Blue Lake, but I've never been there myself. It's very private."

"Why the secrecy?"

"Blue Lake doesn't want to be become a spectacle, some sort of news or social media story. That kind of attention would zap the hope and privacy that these people so desperately need and deserve."

"But how do people learn about Blue Lake? People that have been told they are terminal?"

"Remember the health committee I told you about?"

"Yes."

"I think some of those doctors tell their patients, and some of the patients tell other friends, but only if needed. It's a very closely guarded secret. And you asked about money. From what I understand, the rents and home prices and all of that aren't that different from any other town. I think the founders, and, *no, I don't know who they are*, are not motivated by money. Does that make *any* sense?"

"No and yes, I guess. But, why would Dad move to Blue Lake?"

"Only he can answer that question, Meg. Good luck to you."

"Thanks, Spencer. I really appreciate everything you've told me."

Hi, Dad. Sorry Brian and I had to leave so quickly. Been busy preparing for work. Love you.

Hi, Meg. Glad to hear from you. Was worried. I'm coming to Chicago this weekend. Staying with Rick, Lara, and the kids. Want to visit with you, too. And Brian, of course.

I'll be there.

I can do nothing but stare out the window of my apartment building. I am numb, my brain working on overdrive to process everything Spencer told me. And what

Dad has to say. There can only be one explanation that makes any sense as to why Dad moved to Blue Lake.

Dad is dying.

Chapter 31

"Welcome back, Meg!" says Kelsey.

"We've missed you so much," says Tom. He greets with me with a warm bear hug.

"Please tell Alice thank you for the lasagna. It was delicious and very thoughtful."

"I'll tell her. And take it easy here, kid. No need to jump into anything too big."

"Thanks, Tom."

"The place hasn't been the same without you," says Jerry as he stops at my desk on his way to his office. "There's a story about a new bakery opening in Schiller Park that employs veterans. Why don't you take that assignment and bring back some snacks—on me?"

"You don't have to baby me, Jerry. I can handle real news," I say though I appreciate his intent.

"No babying going on. It's a slow news day, and you know how I like baked goods." He pats his stomach and smiles.

"Take Tom with you."

"Okay, thanks."

The welcome I'm receiving feels good. Brian and I are still lying low at work though Jerry has been fully informed about our relationship. We'd had to sign some papers from human resources about not taking company time on relationship matters or something like that. I'm confident there's a solid place here for Brian *and* me.

My station phone rings. It's Officer Toby, Dad's friend. "Hi, Meg. Glad to hear you are back at work."

"Thanks, Toby."

"How's your dad? I haven't talked to him in a few months."

"He's doing okay. I'll tell him you asked about him."

"Great. Got a minute?"

"Yeah, sure. Everyone is treating me like a baby today, so life is easy." I shrug.

"Good to hear. You've gone through some…stuff."

He has no idea the stuff I've been through that has nothing to do with my mugging at the train platform.

"I have some news about your case."

"Oh?" I sit up in my chair. I honestly haven't given *my case* much thought as I've been so preoccupied with Dad, and my wounds are almost healed.

"We've arrested two of the four individuals we believe to have been the boys on tape that assaulted you."

"Boys?"

"Unfortunately—fifteen and sixteen."

I'm not sure how to process that news. "They're just kids."

"Kids with a lot of baggage, but it doesn't make what they did to you any less serious. They'll be tried as adults."

"Really?"

"Meg, you could have died if you'd hit that pavement differently or if they'd used even a fraction of more force when they hit you in the head. I've seen the evidence. I have the pictures of what you looked like when you were found."

My stomach tightens. I feel like I might throw up. I move my trash can between my legs.

"Are you still there?"

"I am. What happens next?"

"The young men will be arraigned at the courthouse and remanded to the county jail until trial."

"Will I have to testify?"

"Probably not. I think they will take pleas. The evidence is pretty clear from the video at the train stop.

Plus, we're hoping they snitch on the identity of the other guys."

"Okay, thanks, Toby."

"My pleasure. Be well out there."

I check the time. It's almost lunch. I text Brian.

Meet me on the roof for lunch.

I pass Jessalyn on my way to the elevator. She smiles, but it's not for me. Brian steps to my side. He ignores her. "Hey."

"Hey," he says.

"She still has a thing for you, you know?"

"Jessa?" He turns around to see her still following his every move. "She'll have a long wait. Is everything okay? Have you heard from your dad or Spencer again?"

I'd filled Brian in on my conversation with Spencer at dinner last night. He'd taken me to a Chinese restaurant in La Grange. His fortune had said *Financial gain is in you future*. My fortune had said nothing. My fortune cookie was empty. Brian had said it's because I already have everything in my life I could possibly need.

I shake my head *no*. "I haven't talked with them." We look for a place in the shade as summer in July in Chicago in the middle of the day is the worst time to be on the roof of a skyscraper, but I knew we'd have privacy. We sit at a table under a tiny piece of shade from the roofline. Brian takes off his sports coat and loosens his tie. "Damn, it's hot up here."

"Is that all?" I ask.

"Huh?"

"You're not going to say something like, *It's so hot up here because of your giant muscles or some other praise of yourself?* You're losing your touch."

Brian's lips curve upward as he snorts. "It's nice to see you happy again. Sorry I'm a little slow with my vanity today. I've been worried about you."

"I appreciate that. I do. And I guess you have a sixth sense because Officer Toby just called."

"About your case?"

"Yes. They've arrested two of the four guys who attacked me." I pause and close my eyes, wishing I could shut out all of the bad news of this world. "Brian, they are *babies!* Fifteen and sixteen."

"That sucks."

"Yep."

"But they should be held responsible regardless of…"

I put my finger to his lips. "I know. Can we sit here for a minute…together? Without talking?" My mind is tired.

Brian leans against the railing of the rooftop deck. I back up closer to him and lean my head against his chest. He holds me like this for the rest of lunch, neither of us eating a thing.

For the rest of the afternoon I make a list of things I'd want to do if I knew I were dying. The people of Blue Lake created a community with so much warmth. Sharing the experience of learning you are going to die with hundreds of other people who'd been delivered the same news must be powerful. And add to that the collective hope that something in this shared community could offer healing even if it were only the *hope* of that healing that was real. I get it now. Kind of. Maybe. But I certainly understand the need to protect its sacredness.

I finish my list along with an outline that I deliver to Jerry's desk. I have the idea for my next feature story.

Chapter 32

We skip the city's Fourth of July fireworks show in favor of celebrating my birthday with a cozy night in at Brian's condo. We can see fireworks from various municipalities as well as individuals' private shows from their backyards while we sit on his balcony. We sip margaritas and eat too many chips with salsa. It's perfect.

"Why are you staring at me?" I ask Brian who has locked eyes with my lips after I've taken a long sip of margarita.

"I was thinking."

"About what?"

"I've never had sex with a woman in her thirties."

"Oh, really?" I take another drink.

"And did you know that I've never *had* sex as a woman in her thirties?"

"Are you at all curious about seeing if things still work?" He grins and leans back in his chair. A burst of red and yellow lights shoots off in the distance behind his head.

"I'd throw something at you right now if there was something on this balcony to throw."

"But, seriously, should we go see if everything functions the same?"

I stick out my tongue. "You are gross and ridiculous," I say but I can't stop laughing. "And you're also hot."

"Then the answer is *yes*?" His eyes are dancing as the city lights reflect off them.

I stand up first as Brian follows me into the condo. We don't even make it to the bedroom before we rip our clothes off in an eagerness of passion I fully give in to. And I forget all about the fireworks outside because the fireworks show *inside* is more explosive than anything I've felt in my life. Thirty isn't so bad after all.

Chapter 33

Lara is makeup-less when I arrive at her house on Saturday morning. My perfectly put together sister is a mess. I feel sorry for her. I'm sad, too, knowing that Dad is on his way to tell us that he is dying. But I've had more time to process the news because I've seen the hope. I've seen *Hope Street* and the waterfalls and what the people experience when they are there. It makes the crushing news to come a bit easier to accept though the idea of a world without my dad is something I will never get used to.

Dad wears his best chipper attitude when he's engulfed by the boys. Rick and Brian get hugs as well as Lara and me. We let Dad be Grandpa for a bit. He drives cars around the living room floor, stopping to cough or clear his throat every few minutes. Lara and I look at each other. He reads Nolan and Owen a book though Blake, who thinks he's too big for Grandpa's lap, still sits nearby to share in this special time. It's so sad that they will have such few opportunities to make memories with Grandpa Paul.

After lunch of Jimmy John's subway sandwiches (I can't blame Lara for not wanting to cook), Rick and Brian take the boys outside for a squirt gun fight while Lara and I sit with Dad on the front porch. Dad rocks with Lara in the swing that is chained to the roof. I sit across from them in an Adirondack chair.

We wait for Dad to speak first, but when he's taken an unnaturally long time to say anything, I put him out of his misery by letting the truth be known. "We already know, Dad," I say quietly.

He looks confused but then nods his head. "You figured it out because you saw the waterfalls?"

"So, you know about my secret, too?" I ask.

"I wasn't in the condo when you and Brian left because I'd been called to a meeting to tell me that my daughter and her friend had violated Blue Lake rules and snuck onto Hope Street."

"But rules without consequences, right?" asks Lara, "because Meg doesn't *live* there."

"Well, she and Brian aren't allowed to visit again."

That riles Lara up. "They can't stop her! We live in *America*."

"They can't stop her legally, that is true."

"But they will ask you to leave," I say quietly, "if I return."

Dad nods *yes*.

"But they can't do that, either. You own that condo," says Lara who is growing more frustrated.

Dad rests his hand on her shoulder. "And there are association laws I'd be violating if I allowed a guest who…"

"who doesn't follow the rules," I finish.

"Well, that's illegal, too. Blue Lake isn't a dictatorship."

Dad reaches for Lara's hand. "The beauty of Blue Lake is the sense of community and support we get from each other. If trust is betrayed, then ugliness festers that can't exist in a community like Blue Lake."

"And the positivity and hope that have been cultivated go out the door."

Dad nods again.

I start to cry. "I'm so sorry, Dad. You were so happy there, and now I've ruined it for you."

"Oh, Meg. You didn't ruin anything. It was killing me not to be able to tell you and Lara why I moved to Blue Lake, what the hope of being healed and *not* having a death sentence hanging over me might mean for our family." Dad pauses and wipes his own eyes. "But it didn't take me long to realize the real power that Blue Lake held." He coughs into his sleeve, my once strong father looking so frail and weak. "Blue Lake is like a living hospice program. For some, living daily in a community of positivity with the freedom to choose to do what makes you happy with others who see the joy in every remaining breath, too, well, for some it extends their quality of life. When I saw ambulances come into town, without sirens blaring, of course, I knew that people were still dying. But I quickly realized they were dying on their own terms—much like at Pine Crest where Mom died—but different, too. Here people were still able to live lives fully boosted by others who wanted desperately to extend their walk on this Earth, too. It works, for some. But, for most, it doesn't. And I'm at peace right now. I have no regrets. I have loved every minute of my time in Blue Lake. I won't trade the hope and joy I experienced there for anything, even if it didn't cure my illness. I lived as if I were in heaven already during my time there, made better by visits with my family, of course."

"Oh, Daddy!" Lara wraps her arms around Dad. We sit on the porch on a sunny, warm day in July when the world around us is barbequing and swimming and playing, and we cry. For a long time.

Chapter 34

On a crisp September morning, we lay Dad to rest next to Mom at a pretty cemetery on a hill that overlooks Lake Michigan. They are together again, and for me, that gives great peace. There are people at the cemetery I do not know though I am not surprised. Dad lived an active life. His impact on others will never be fully known. Lara takes five yellow roses from the top of the casket flower spread before she leaves, one for each member of her sweet family. The boys seem lost, not able to understand what has happened to their beloved grandpa. I take two roses, one for Brian and me. Dad loved him almost as much as me. He'd told me that the last day he was conscious at Pine Crest, where he'd chosen to go when he became too sick.

"143, Dad," I say as I touch the casket one last time.

Brian puts his arm around me as we walk to the car to go back to life, which seems at this moment more like it's something oblique that happens *around* me instead of *to* me.

"Excuse me. Are you Meg?"

I turn around to see a man with a full beard and a gentle smile. He looks familiar, but I've met so many new people the last two days. "Yes."

"Hello—again. I'm sorry to be meeting under another unpleasant set of circumstances."

"Again?"

"Sorry. You might not remember me. It was dark after all."

I wrinkle my forehead. I'm so tired. I just want to go home. "I'm sorry. I don't remember you."

"It's okay. I was rather grumpy."

"Oh!" I hear Brian say next to me. "You're the guy from the yard by the waterfall—in Blue Lake."

"I am," the man says solemnly.

"If you came here to warn me not to make trouble, you don't have to worry," I say. "I won't out the secret of Blue Lake. I understand what the community offers people. I get it. Please don't yell at me. I'm not in…"

The man puts a gentle hand on my arm. "Meg, I'm not here to yell at you. In fact, I am here to thank you and to honor your wonderful father."

"But…I…"

"You caused quite a stir with all of your snooping—both of you." He looks at Brian. "But what you did changed things in Blue Lake."

"Go on," says Brian who is holding me up as my strength has depleted.

"Your messing around and finding out about the waterfalls nearly shut the town down."

"Look, sir, this doesn't help now. You have our assurances that we won't tell anyone."

"No, no, please. Hear me out. It was your dad who convinced the board that sending family members to Blue Lake under the premise that absolutely no one in the family can know the real reason why is, well, is cruel. Husbands were leaving wives to come to Blue Lake and only visit their loved ones on the weekends. And wives were leaving husbands. Fathers left children back home. Mothers did the same. Even children, sometimes barely legal adults, would move hours away to Blue Lake, and always in the wake of these moves there'd be turmoil and mistrust and pain. Families didn't understand. That's why you went to the extremes that you did to find out what makes Blue Lake so…special. Your dad explained *why* you'd been asking questions and trying to see what was at the end of Hope

Street. Your dad didn't hold back about his real thoughts. He gave quite an impassioned speech about how the families deserved a chance to believe in hope, too. So, the board changed their rules—though it wasn't easy. Families, at least those who *have* to know, *can* know why their loved ones move to Blue Lake. Not everyone gets it, but so far the secret hasn't leaked."

"And the hope on Hope Street lives on," I say, smiling for the first time in days.

"Yes, Meg. The hope in Blue Lake lives on. You did that, you and your husband."

"Boyfriend," I say. I look at Brian. He is smiling, too.

Chapter 35

Jerry had eagerly accepted my proposed feature story. It's running tonight. After work, the station employees who are still here after the 10:00 news are going to Henry's to celebrate. My story runs at 6:00.

"Are you nervous?" Jessalyn asks me as I sit at my desk tapping my pen up and down on my computer keyboard.

"Not really."

"Well, despite the fact that you *look* like you're nervous, you shouldn't be. You're a fine reporter, Meg, and you're going places." She smiles—kind of.

"Uh, thanks, Jessa."

"And I told Jerry that he should consider you for the new mid-day program the station is piloting in a few months."

Chicago Midday. I am well aware of the new program. "Thanks, Jessa. But why don't you want the host job?"

"Me? No, I rely on the teleprompter too much. You said so yourself. Ha! Plus, I'll have a hot new co-anchor in a couple of weeks."

"Look, Jessa, Brian and I are a couple. I'm sorry if you still thi…"

"Brian? Good land, I'm waaaayyyy over him. I'm leaving WDOU for the station down the road, and from what I hear, Ross Reynelds is newly single." Jessalyn turns on her three inch heels and walks away.

"And now for this week's feature story from our own star reporter, Meg Popkin: *Knocking Out That Bucket List Without Regrets.*"

"Thanks, Brian. That's right, how many times have you caught yourself saying, *I'll do it tomorrow?* Or *There's time for this next week.* The sad reality is that the average lifespan has decreased since the times of Covid, so why should we put off until later what we could be doing now? I've reached out to fellow Chicagoland residents to find out what is on their bucket lists, and you might be surprised…."

"To Meg!" Jerry says as he raises his glass in a toast at Henry's.

I blush, my face as warm as my heart. "Thanks, Jerry. Thank for the opportunity to tell another story that *I* really wanted to tell."

"You told it well, and I'm sure the numbers will show the same."

"Must it always be about the numbers with you?" I shake my head. And I know the answer is *yes*.

"If those numbers come through, it's another notch in your resume for Jessa's job. You and Brian would make quite a team on the anchor desk. How about it? Want to apply?"

Jerry towers over me, and I feel small, but I am confident in my answer. "No, thanks. I don't want a traditional anchor job, but I might ask for a recommendation for the *Chicago Midday Show*."

"You've got it, Meg." He hugs me and goes to the bar to order another round of drinks.

"Meg, can I come to the show with you if you get the job? Anita would kill me if I didn't get to see you every day and have someone to give leftovers to." Tom grabs a handful of pretzels.

And Kelsey laughs loudly—too loudly.

"Oh, Tom. How could I possibly turn down that request if Alice's leftovers are included?"

It feels great to be with so many people who care about me, but the one I care about the most is very quiet.

He stands next to a high-top table taking in the scene. The station has commandeered five tables. Bottles of beer sit on the tables amongst the bowls of pretzels and popcorn. Jerry and Tom start a game of darts. Kelsey and the traffic reporter discuss the best strategies for solving Wordle puzzles. Brian seems to take it all in. He's wearing a red shirt with a picture of a blue lake, a nice nod to my dad and the craziness at the end of his life. I really miss him.

"What are you thinking about, Mr. Serious?" I ask.

"I'm just living life."

"Hmm…that's kind of deep," I say, snuggling in close to his side.

Brian stares down at me, his green eyes swimming with something that looks like contentment. "Well, you see, I just heard this great report on the news tonight…"

"You said that it was on tonight?" I ask playfully.

"Yes, on a little station called WDOU. Maybe you've heard of it?"

"Uh-huh. I believe I have."

"So, anyway this really cute lady, like *really cute*, told me that I need to live my life to the fullest when I can and not put off until tomorrow what I should be doing today."

"Ooh, that sounds interesting." I kiss Brian on the cheek. "Tell me more."

At that moment, Brian takes the spoon from the popcorn bowl and bangs his beer bottle. *"Quiet, please."*

I just stare, unsure what is happening. Brian commands an audience by his handsome appearance alone, but when his booming voice starts talking, everyone stops what they are doing and turns to look at him.

"We are here tonight to celebrate Meg Popkin on the continuance of a great career. I think we can all agree that she has a bright future." *Here! Here!* says someone from behind him. "And in the spirit of Meg's story, it's time to do something tonight I'd been waiting to do in a few weeks. But why wait? We are only promised a finite number of days. We should live them to the fullest."

My heart quickens, and my eyes fill with tears.

Brian drops to his knee and grabs hold of my hand so that I am facing him. "Meggin Popkin, *Meg*, you've shown me what love looks like. You put up with my crap, and you still love me. You make me a better person. And—since everyone already thinks I'm your husband," People around us laugh. "would you do me the honor of *actually* making me your husband and marry me?"

I fling my arms around his neck before he's even finished asking me the question. "Yes, yes! I'll marry you." I don't even wipe away the tears that now freely fall.

"Cheers! Another round of drinks on me!" yells Jerry. The crowd erupts in applause, for the free beer—and for Brian and me.

"I think you forgot something!" Tom yells from the dartboard line.

"Oh! Crap! Meg, here. I'm sorry!"

"What a goofball," says Kelsey as Brian pulls out the ring box.

"Yep, but he's my goofball." Brian slides a beautiful pear cut diamond ring with two smaller adjoining diamonds, one on each side, onto my ring finger.

"It's beautiful," I whisper as I let him hold me close.

He whispers in my ear. "The diamonds on the side are from your dad. Well, I mean, he gave me a diamond ring of your mothers, and I used two of the diamonds to place in your engagement ring."

"Does that mean that Dad knew you were going to ask me to marry you?"

"Of course, silly girl. You don't think I didn't talk to him about marrying you, do you?"

"But he died months ago."

"And I've known for much longer." He tenderly kisses my lips. And in a sea of people, we are alone. It's the greatest feeling in the world.

The Sequel to The Secret of Blue Lake: available August 2023

The Secret of Silver Beach (2)

After solving the mystery of the secret of Blue Lake, Meg returns to Chicago and to her new job as co-host on Chicago Midday. But when poor chemistry with Trenton Dealy leads to problems on the show, Meg is assigned a travel segment that will send her on location all around Lake Michigan visiting beach towns and local tourist attractions. The trip takes her away from fiancé Brian who has to continue anchoring the nightly news in Chicago. When odd threats start hurtling in Meg's direction, she finally confesses to Brian and those closest to her that she might have a stalker. Do the threats have something to do with the new information she learned about her Dad's past in the little town of St. Joseph, Michigan, or is there something bigger at play that threatens more than Meg's livelihood?

Chapter 1

"What's on tap today, Meg?" Brian asks as he sits up in bed, rubbing his eyes.

I watch him reach his arms up in what can only be described as a sexy stretch, but I have more important things to do than stare at my fiancé as he gets out of bed. "I'm interviewing a child about her fundraising idea to raise money for childhood cancers. She's making custom-colored bracelets to sell through her online Etsy store. She's the number one storefront in her genre. It's really quite amazing."

"Sounds cool."

"And there's the typical holiday-related stories, of course."

"Are on-air costumes in your future, my little princess?" Brian asks as he jumps back into bed and plants a kiss on my forehead.

I push him off playfully. "Unfortunately, I'm learning all sorts of things about the differences in reporting news at a major Chicago news station versus hosting a midday show."

"Co-hosting," Brian smiles.

I throw a pillow at him and walk to the bathroom. "I'd like to forget about that part."

Trenton Dealy. I thought Brian was cocky when I first met him at WDOU, but compared to working with Trenton, the early days of work with Brian were like being with an overly excited—but sweet—puppy.

"Be tough, Meg. Don't give him the satisfaction of seeing you upset. You've had practice dealing with arrogance," Brian winks at me. "I'm going to shower at the gym. See you tonight. Have a great day." He kisses me on the cheek, grabs an apple, and heads out the door of his condo. Soon we will condo hunt for our own place, and I can't wait for the day when we aren't living out of duffle bags as we move back and forth between Brian's downtown condo and my apartment in the Chicago suburbs.

I still take the "L" train to the studio like I used to do when I worked at WDOU. I wouldn't say that I'm afraid, but ever since I was assaulted and robbed earlier in the year, I'm definitely more aware of my surroundings. I wear a small cross-body purse that I grip tightly and a whistle around my neck. I don't like living like a fearful animal, but PTSD is real; so the more prepared I can be, the easier it is for me to travel on the train. And even though the four teenagers who attacked me have all been arrested and taken plea deals putting them in prison for years, I still can't help but wonder if their friends are out there and waiting to attack again.

"Hi, Meg," says Becca as I slide into the chair for my hair and makeup, which is a much bigger deal for a co-hosting job than for a reporter. There are perks to this job.

"Hey, Becca. Sorry I didn't have time to stop for coffee this morning."

"No worries. I'll drink the station coffee," she laughs.

"I hope you don't choke on the coffee grounds."

"I'll be sure to sue the company if I do."

Her smile lights up the room, and I'm reminded that there *are* good people that work with me at Chicago Midday. Tom followed me from WDOU, too, so having my favorite camera operator on the other side of the camera every day is another positive benefit, although I think he misses running with a camera on his shoulder or at his side. Standing behind a stationary camera is a new skill. Plus, I think he's put on a few pounds from not getting all those extra steps running around the city. I certainly won't be the one to tell him that, though.

"Have you seen the call sheet for the Halloween show on Friday?" Becca asks.

"Not yet. Trenton and I have a meeting with Char today. It must be bad if hair and makeup got advance notice." I raise an eyebrow in question.

Becca nods her head. "Oh, it's most definitely going to be a busy hair and makeup day." She grins evilly and puts a finger to her mouth. "But I will let Char break the news to you."

I roll my eyes and take a deep breath. I remind myself that I took this job because it gives me more latitude to dive into stories that are most important to me such as my hospice story and my bucket list story at WDOU. I am not limited by minutes-long time constraints for storytelling at Chicago Midday. I can go in depth and ask the questions that I want to ask. But the trade-off is having to do silly things such as eat unusual foods or learn hip hop dance moves or wear Halloween costumes *on camera* and live in front of thousands of people.

"All done," says Becca.

I look in the mirror one last time before heading to my meeting with Char. My eyes shine much too brightly for the morning hours, but I can't deny that Becca and her techniques make me look prettier and more sophisticated than my thirty years of age. My shoulder-length brown hair hangs straight today but shines with health and no frizz. Becca is a miracle worker.

"Thanks, Becca. I'll bring you a mocha tomorrow morning as long as you're still here—you know, assuming that you don't choke on those coffee grounds from the coffee maker today."

"I can only hope for the best. Have a great day, Meg!"

"Someone needs a watch," I hear when I walk into Char's office.

"Good morning to you, too, Trenton," I say through gritted teeth.

"Hair and makeup are taking longer and longer every day, Meg. Perhaps you should help Becca out and do some moisturizing of your face and eyebrow plucking *before* you come to work. That would likely save her a lot of time."

"Really?"

"I'm serious. I'm only looking out for you, Meg." He smiles, his giant eyes nearly popping off his face. But I can't deny that those eyes translate well on a television screen.

"Play nice, kids," says Char as she walks into the room and takes a seat behind her large black desk. Char's purple stripe in her black hair matches her office chair.

"Meg knows I am only teasing." Trenton flashes a quick smile in my direction.

"It's a big week," says Char.

"That might be an understatement," I say to the producer of Chicago Midday.

"Although everything is a *first* this year, we anticipate that our Halloween show on Friday will bring big ratings. People will tune in just to see the costumes that the two of you are wearing. Plus, we've got holiday cooking segments and decoration making and new music from Alaban. Busy, busy, busy!" She smiles through her stress. She thrives off the chaos of producing a new midday show in a large viewing market. Char flips her chin-length hair behind her ears and puts on her reading glasses. "Meg, I need you to meet with Danni about the cooking segment for today's show. She will walk you through what you will be doing. Trenton, there's a police officer coming in to discuss a new neighborhood watch program in the city. I've sent you an email about talking points."

"Char," I say, interrupting, "Who's the officer? I had a lot of contacts when I worked at WDOU. Maybe I could take that story."

Trenton starts waving his arms wildly in the air. "Hold on a minute here. Meg doesn't get all the feel-good stories just because she's a girl. I can handle the police officer."

I glare at him. "First of all, I'm a *woman*, not a *girl*. Secondly, it's not a feel-good story. It's an important story about limiting crime in the city through the help of its citizens. And I was just saying that…"

"Just because *you've* been a crime victim doesn't mean you should get all of the crime stories. Damn, Meg. You are really going to milk your assault for as long as you can, aren't you?"

I ball my fingers into a fist. I have never wanted to hit someone as much as I want to hit Trenton Dealy right now.

"Stop it, you two. I told you to play nice. I've given you your assignments. When you are done with them, you both need to meet sometime today with Clive. He's going to fit you for your costumes on Friday. I am not kidding, though." She looks from Trenton to me with a stern look on her face. "If you two don't improve your attitude with each other, this show is going to fail, and then we are all out of jobs. The audience can sense chemistry, and yours is sorely lacking, especially here. Pretty soon you won't be able to hide it on air if you don't work on your relationship *off the air*. That is why…." She takes a deep breath. "That is why I have signed you up for an escape room."

"What the hell is that?" Trenton asks before I can.

"It's a room with puzzles and activities you have to solve together. You have a time limit, so in order to *win* the game you have to work with each other within a set amount of time."

"You can't be serious?" I ask. It may be the first time Trenton and I have agreed on anything since we began working at Chicago Midday a month ago.

"I am very serious. I worked hard to get this program approved. It was years in the making. You were each chosen for your unique skill sets. I'll be damned if I will let you two prove me wrong because your egos are too big to coexist, so if you need practice working together productively, then practice you will get. You are scheduled to be at this address tonight at 5:30 p.m. Don't be late and *don't* fail this challenge."

*****

I would like to extend a heartfelt thanks to Betty for being the first person to read The Secret of Blue Lake and for giving me her guidance and expertise. Thank you to Heather, Keri, and Cindy for being fantastic, encouraging readers of an early draft of this book. I am quite fortunate to have trusted and wise friends.

Thank you to Ed, Connor, and Luke for always encouraging me to pursue my passions. The house is much too quiet now, but I do appreciate the writing time.

Printed in Great Britain
by Amazon